CONNECTED TO THE PLUG 2

DWAN WILLIAMS

Good2Go Publishing

CONNECTED TO THE PLUG 2
Written by Dwan Williams
Cover Design: Davida Baldwin
Typesetter: Mychea
ISBN: 9781943686384
Copyright ©2017 Good2Go Publishing
Published 2017 by Good2Go Publishing
7311 W. Glass Lane • Laveen, AZ 85339
www.good2gopublishing.com
https://twitter.com/good2gobooks
G2G@good2gopublishing.com
www.facebook.com/good2gopublishing
www.instagram.com/good2gopublishing

ACKNOWLEDGMENT

First and foremost, I would like to thank God; my mother, Carolyn J. Williams; my sister, Carolyn N. Williams-Gorham; my brother, Alex Williams; my aunt Mary; cousins Erica, Sawanda, Demorris, and Shay; my entire family in New Jersey and the DC area; K. Floyd; S. Harper; my friends on lock; and to everyone who loved and supported me throughout my journey as a writer. I can't forget the woman who inspires me every day, my late great-grandmother, Georgiana Williams-Barnes, and all of my fans and followers. You will not be disappointed in *Connected to the Plug: Part II*.

Last but definitely not least, I would like to acknowledge Good2Go Publishing for believing in my ability to write as an author, giving me this great opportunity to bring to you my creative style of writing, and also for helping me bring my dream as an author to a reality.

I almost forgot! To all my frenemies, non-believers, and haters, I would like to say: I MADE IT!

PEACE . . .

Two Years Later

"**This** is the best Christmas ever!" Speedy cheered as he pulled into the parking lot of the Eastern Carolina Rehabilitation Center in Green-ville, North Carolina.

Fuzzy looked over at her husband and smiled. She hadn't seen him that excited since the day they got married, or when she delivered their beautiful daughter, Sadé, into the world.

"Look at your boy! He's still the same old Menace!" Fuzzy laughed.

She watched him flirt with the nurses as he stood in front of the rehab center. When he noticed Speedy's G55 pull up in front of him, he threw up his arms in the air.

"My nigga!" Menace called out after saying his goodbyes

to the ladies as Speedy got out from the driver's side to assist him with his luggage.

Even though Menace was happy to be leaving, he was going to miss the late-night massages he had been getting when the nurses came in and checked up on him. The extra attention was thanks for the hefty tips Speedy used to pay them for making sure his partner was comfortable as possible during his stay. Fuzzy noticed one of the nurses staring at Speedy too long, and he decided it was time to go.

"You need to hurry up, bae, before one of these witches gets their head split," she warned as the limo tint of the Benz truck came down revealing her presence.

After the nurse stormed off in the direction of the rehab center's entrance, Menace laughed and then hopped in the backseat.

"Oh shit! This how y'all doing it now, big timers?" he joked while looking at the ceiling of the truck and all of the head rests, and admiring the many televisions playing his favorite movie. "Yo! Turn that up a little. This my part."

Fuzzy turned the volume up as Speedy got in the driver's seat.

"No coke? What do you mean there's no coke? I search everywhere, there's no fuckin' coke!" Menace shouted as the DVD played *The Usual Suspect*.

Fuzzy shook her head as Speedy pulled out of the parking lot into traffic and headed back to Wilson.

"So, this how y'all doing it now?" Menace asked again when they got on Highway 264.

All Speedy could do was smile at how far he had come since the last time Menace was on the scene.

"You ain't seen nothing yet!" he boasted, before cutting his eyes over at Fuzzy.

Menace sat up between the front seat and looked in Fuzzy's face.

"So, what's up, sis? You been keeping my partner in place?" Menace questioned.

"Of course," she replied while popping her collar. "You know me."

Speedy sucked his teeth and curled his lips before snickering. "Anyway!" he interjected before Fuzzy playfully punched him in the arm.

They laughed and joked like old times all the way back to the city limits.

"I remember this place," Menace said out loud when they pulled into the parking lot of Big Mama's Kitchen.

Speedy knew Menace wouldn't be able to remember each and every place that they used to frequent, but he was glad to know he remembered their favorite restaurant. They parked in front of the entrance, got out of the truck, and then made their way into the establishment.

"Welcome home," everyone in the place cheered all together once Menace walked in the doorway.

Menace turned around with a smile on his face and looked at Speedy and Fuzzy. Fuzzy held her phone up in his face and

4

took a picture to capture the moment of a lifetime.

"Y'all didn't have to do all of this."

"We didn't!" Fuzzy replied to him as she pointed behind his back.

"I did it," Red admitted.

By the time Menace turned completely around, she jumped dead into his arms and kissed him on his lips. Even though she visited him every week, he was happy to have her in his arms at that moment. He couldn't wait to get her home and make love to her all night long.

"Okay. Okay. Come on, lovebirds. Let's go to our table," Fuzzy instructed as she then led the way to the booth in the far corner that was set up just for them.

After everyone was seated and bottles were popped, Speedy stood to his feet to make a toast. "I want to thank all of you for coming out and joining us on this joyous occasion to celebrate the return of one of the realist niggas to ever grace the ill streets of Wilson," he announced, before looking down at his long-time partner and best friend.

Menace bowed his head gracefully, and then held his champagne bottle in the air.

"This man has been gone a long time. So long that most of you don't know who he is. For you that don't know, let me fill you in. His name is Menace. He and I started this crew from nothing, and now we have it all. I want all of you to treat him with the same trust, respect, loyalty, and honor that y'all treat me and Fuzzy with."

Red cleared her throat to get Speedy's attention.

"My fault, Red," he laughed before continuing. "Also Red," he added, before getting back on a serious note. Speedy looked around to meet all of the onlookers' stares. He continued after being sure he had everyone's undivided attention. "If there's anyone that has any objections to what I just said, you can leave now," Speedy pointed to the door.

The building was so quiet you could hear an ant piss on cotton. When no one moved, Fuzzy popped the cork from her bottle of Moscato and then held it in the air.

"To Menace," she yelled as suds ran down her bottle onto her arms.

"To Menace," the crowd roared in unison, all popping the tops of their bottles as well.

Menace stood to his feet and looked around. He couldn't believe that their once four-man crew had grown into a small army of niggers. He just hoped that their hearts matched their rugged demeanor.

"We made it to the top, my nigga!" Speedy whispered in Menace's ear as he walked over to his side.

"Say cheese," Fuzzy screamed, before she then took a picture of the duo.

"It's time to party," Red yelled out when the DJ put on *I'm Getting' Money* by OJ Da Juiceman.

Menace thought back to the first time he met Red at The Twilight Zone. He knew he was in for the time of his life when she dragged him to the middle of the dance floor and dropped it like it was hot. Everything started to move in slow motion for him as he looked around at everyone having a good time. The crowd began to cheer his and Red's names as they did their thing. He couldn't believe that a little over a year and a half ago he was in the hospital fighting for his life; and now he was having the time of his life with a beautiful woman in front of him. The strange thing of it all was that he still felt like he was missing something or someone. He had stayed up plenty of nights with the image of another woman in his mind. He couldn't quite see her clearly, but he knew he loved her.

"You okay?" Red asked, once she noticed Menace standing there in a daze.

"You want to go sit down?" Menace managed to put on a smile, grab her hand, and head back to the booth.

Before they could make it across the floor, Speedy put his hand on Red's shoulder. "Sorry, but I need to borrow your boo for a minute," he shouted over the loud music.

"A'ight, Speedy. Don't make me come lookin' for y'all," she joked, before throwing her hands the air.

"Fuzzy!" she called out, before heading to their booth to join her.

Speedy led the way to the office in the back so he could speak with Menace in private.

"You enjoying yourself, playboy?" he asked, before taking a seat behind the cherry desk facing the door.

"No doubt, homie!" Menace smiled.

"What's on your mind?" Speedy asked, sensing that something was bothering him.

"You swear you know me," Menace laughed before continuing. "It ain't nothing really. I might be just trippin' or something, but I keep picturing this girl in my head."

Speedy took another swallow of his champagne and then exhaled. He knew the time would come when Menace would ask about Crystal. He just didn't know exactly how he was going to explain things.

"You're probably talking about Crystal, your ex," he began. "You might wanna grab that chair," Speedy said, pointing to the chair in the corner.

Menace took a seat in front of the desk and braced himself for the news he was about to receive.

"Crystal and my ex, Tawana, were sisters. Tawana hooked y'all up about a month or so after her and I got together. You and Crystal lived together. As a matter of fact, she was the one that found you shot and called the ambulance and then me. That was right before Tawana and our son—!" Speedy paused as he thought about their untimely deaths. "I meant Tawana and her son," he corrected himself before he continued. "After that, Crystal packed up and then left town with your Jag and the safe," Speedy said as he shrugged his shoulders. "No note, no phone call, no explanation! Nothing!"

Speedy looked into his partner's eyes and saw the anger deep within them as Menace bit down on his bottom lip to control his emotions.

"No matter what may be going through your head right now, she did love you," he confirmed. "She even—!"

"Fuck that bitch!" Menace interrupted and stood to his feet, knocking his chair on its side.

Speedy sat silently as Menace vented his pain.

"If she loved me, she would've stayed by my side and never would've stolen from me. Now I got nothing," Menace said as he began to pace the floor with thoughts of how to seek revenge for her betrayal. "I'ma kill that bitch," he vowed, before smashing his fist into the palm of his hand.

"Chill, homie! Don't even trip on that petty shit. All that's in the past. We run this city now," Speedy proclaimed as he then took the last sip from his champagne bottle and rounded the desk.

The sound of the knock on the door broke their stare.

"I told y'all I would come looking for you if you kept my boo too long." Red smiled as she entered the room. She could sense the tension in the air as she stood to the side between them. "You ready to go home, baby?"

"I'll be ready in two minutes," Menace replied as he turned to face her.

"Two minutes!" she verified, before giving him a kiss and then exiting the same way she entered.

Once Red closed the door behind her, Speedy continued where he left off. "Look, homie! You don't have to sweat her or the money," he promised before walking to the closet and returning with a black leather briefcase that he set it on top of the desk.

Menace's mouth fell wide open when he opened it up. Inside was $200,000 all in $100 bills.

"Welcome home, partner!"

Menace was at a loss of words as he took a stack out and thumbed through it.

"That should be enough to hold you over until we get up later on in the week to discuss your position in our organization," Speedy assured him as he walked up beside him and gave him a pat on his back. "You ain't seen nothing yet."

Menace looked up at his partner as a smile crept up on his face, before embracing him and then heading back to the party.

"Where's Red at?" Speedy asked Fuzzy, once they made it back to the table.

"She's outside at the car waiting for Menace. Is everything all right," she asked with concern.

"No doubt," Menace answered as he grabbed his jacket.

He gave Fuzzy a hug and his partner some dap before making his way outside. When he opened up the door, a pearl-white Panamera Turbo with tinted windows pulled up in front of him. He hated the fact he didn't have his gun on him when he reached for his waistline.

"You ready?" Red asked, lowering the window on the passenger's side.

Menace bent down and looked into the car as Red smiled back at him.

"Whose car you driving?" he asked with a confused look on his face.

"It's yours," Speedy announced while walking up behind him. "The big surprise will come tomorrow when I pick you up."

Menace shook his head and then got into the passenger side of his new car.

"Y'all be safe, and don't do nothing I wouldn't do," Fuzzy yelled out from behind Speedy as Red and Menace pulled away from the entrance and out of the parking lot.

~ ~ ~

"You okay, baby?" Fuzzy asked when she came out of the bathroom.

Speedy sat on the bed with the television off, thinking about what the future held for his crew now that his partner was home, as Fuzzy made her way across their room.

"Yeah, I'm good!"

She could tell Speedy had a lot on his mind with Menace coming home and all, but she knew everything would work out fine for him and the crew.

"Don't stress it, baby. Everything's going to work out for the best," she assured him as she walked over to the bed and stood in front of him. "Let me help ease your mind a little bit."

Fuzzy opened her robe, propped her left leg onto the bed, and then opened her vagina with two fingers. Speedy's eyes lit up like a kid in a candy store. After placing several kisses around her love button, he placed it in his mouth and sucked gently before running his tongue on it in a circular motion.

"Give it to me, daddy!" she begged, gripping the back of his head.

Speedy palmed and then lifted her up by her ass cheeks and sat her on his face. She rode his tongue like a natural-born cowgirl, and he enjoyed every minute of it.

Just as promised, Speedy was up and knocking on Red's apartment door first thing in the morning. He was shocked when Menace answered the door fully dressed.

"Man, we got to get you some new gear," Speedy laughed, looking his partner up and down. He pointed at the two-year-old blue jean Akademic suit Menace had on, and bowed over. Speedy remembered when that outfit was one of the fliest sets in the world to him; now he wouldn't be caught dead in it.

"I'm out, baby!" Menace yelled up the steps to Red, ignoring Speedy's annoying laugh.

"All right, baby. Call me when you're on your way home, so I can be here when you get back," she replied, before peeking her head out from the top corner of the stairs and blowing him a kiss.

"Back atcha!" he shouted, before following Speedy out the door.

~ ~ ~

After Speedy took Menace to the mall for an all-out shopping spree, he caught him up on all the latest happenings on the streets.

"What we doing over here?" Menace asked after they entered Buckhorn Estates, where they met up with Ms. Taylor, Speedy's real estate agent.

"I need you to help me pick out a new crib," he informed as they jumped out of Speedy's S550.

After introducing Menace to Ms. Taylor, they looked at the two-story, three-bedroom, two-and-a-half bath, white home with blue shutters outlining the windows.

"How about this one?" Speedy asked Menace as they walked to the side to look at the two-car garage.

The frown on Menace's face let him know what he thought of the place.

17

"Do you have anything with something like a three- or four-car garage?" Menace asked Ms. Taylor as he walked back to the car.

Speedy smiled and shrugged his shoulders.

"As a matter of fact, I do. I think you will love the next house we have to offer," she admitted.

They headed to their cars, and she led the way to the next location a few blocks away. Menace couldn't believe the difference in the residences that two blocks made as he glanced out the windows at the mini mansions. They all ranged from three to four stories in height, and sat on at least two to three acres of land.

"How about this one?" Ms. Taylor asked once Speedy and Menace got out of the car.

Speedy looked at his partner for his approval. Before Menace answered, he walked to the side of the house and saw that it had a four-car garage on the side of it and a barn in the back. Menace nodded his head and then made his way to the barn to look inside.

"Yo! Come check this shit right here out," he yelled out to Speedy.

Speedy made his way to the barn and stuck his head in. He knew how much Menace loved to ride four-wheelers and dirt bikes. He then thought back to when they used to go to the Honda shop and steal all kinds of ATVs and sell them.

"I'm going to have to come over from time to time and whip yo' ass in a little pool," Menace joked as he walked over to the competition-sized pool table and took a practice shot, combining the one to the six ball in the corner pocket. "I still got it," Menace boasted before laying the pool stick back on the table.

"You're gonna need more than one lucky shot to beat me," Speedy replied, before he headed toward the door.

"So I guess this is the one?" Ms. Taylor asked with briefcase in hand, ready to handle all of the necessary paperwork to make the deal final.

Speedy looked over at his partner to see what he had to say about the place. After Menace whispered a couple of words in his ear, Speedy said a few words to the realtor before she handed over the keys, wished him luck on the new place, and then pulled off in her car.

"Yo! I'ma need you to call me later on tonight," Speedy shouted over his shoulders as he threw the house keys in the air.

Menace caught the keys as Speedy hopped in his Benz and started it.

"Yo! How am I getting back home?" Menace laughed, because he thought Speedy was joking around like he usually did.

"Look behind door number one," Speedy instructed, before he pulled out of the driveway and sped off down the street.

Menace just shook his head at how crazy his homie was, and then looked down at the keys in his hands. Menace hit the button that read #1 on the remote, and the first garage door slid up. He smiled when he saw the matching pearl-white Porsche Cayenne Turbo backed up inside of it. Menace stood speechless for a few seconds as he let things sink in.

"It's yours!" Speedy confirmed, once Menace called his cellular.

Before hanging up, Menace swore to pay him back, but Speedy wasn't hearing it.

"What's mine is yours, bruh. If it wasn't for you, none of this would be possible. You and I built this shit, not just me," Speedy said and then ended the call.

He then headed to Pender Street Park to coach the basketball team he had formed, which had been the reigning champions for the last two years running.

On Menace's way back to the apartment to tell Red the good news, he received a call from Speedy telling him to meet him at Pender Street Park before he went in. Since he was just a few blocks away, it only took him about two-and-a-half minutes to get there. Menace sat in his truck for a couple of minutes watching his lil' homie Lucky do his thing as shooting guard. He got out of the truck when he heard Speedy call out his name and wave him courtside.

"I didn't know Lucky was like dat," Menace admitted.

Lucky gave a behind-the-back pass to Lil Man, who shot it with ease over the much taller center they had nicknamed "Tank" because of his big structure.

"But my homie's better," Speedy laughed as the red team took the ball out of bounds.

"So you trying to make a bet that my man Lucky's gonna score more points than Lil Man?" Menace asked his partner.

Speedy always loved a good challenge, so he bet a $500 wager on the little homies. It was the last point of the game, and Lucky brought the ball down full speed.

He pointed to Menace and mouthed the words, "This one's for you!" He then made a swift crossover to the left, making his opponent stumble right as he then flew right by him. Just as he was about to go up for the winning layup, Tank came out of nowhere and elbowed him in his side and made him lose the ball.

"Oh, hell naw!" Menace shouted, before he ran onto the court and caught Tank in the jaw, dropping him to the ground.

"Yo! What are you doing?" Speedy asked as he ran up behind Menace and pulled him away. "He's with us."

"It's okay, big homie!" Lucky confirmed as he stood back up to his feet.

Menace looked down at Tank. "My fault, lil' homie. I didn't know." Menace offered Tank a hand to help him up, but Tank brushed it off.

"It ain't a thang," he responded, before wiping the dirt off his arm.

Menace pulled out a $100 bill to show there were no hard feelings, but Tank declined the gesture.

"You need to put four more with that one and pay your debt," Speedy joked. "While y'all baby-sat Lucky, Lil Man scored the winning basket, making him one point over Lucky."

Menace laughed as he pulled out four more $100 bills and handed them over. Speedy then counted off two of the $100 bills and handed them to Lil Man.

"I'll meet y'all back at the spot a little later," Menace told the crew.

After showing everyone some love, he jumped back in his truck and headed to the apartment to pick up Red and show her their new house.

~ ~ ~

"Surprise!" Red tried her best to focus her eyes as quickly as she could once Menace removed the blindfolds, eager to see what had him so hyped up.

"This is so beautiful," she admitted as she made her way further into the spacious foyer.

She admired the huge fountain that sat in the middle of the set of staircases that led to the second floor. It reminded

24

her of Menace's favorite movie, *Scarface*. The only thing that was missing was the "The World Is Mine" sign.

"You ain't seen nothing yet," Menace claimed full of excitement, snapping Red from her thoughts.

Before she could get a word out, Menace was on his way to what she later found out was the east wing of the mini mansion.

"You ready for this?" Menace asked once Red was by his side.

Without waiting for her to respond, he opened the double doors. Red's mouth almost hit the floor as Menace led her down the aisle leading to the front of the room where a theater screen hung. By the time she made it up front, she had counted twenty seats on each side of the aisle. Menace put a finger under Red's chin to close her mouth as he then turned on his heels and headed back up the aisle to the exit.

"Come on!" he rushed her, ready to take her to the west wing to show her the next big surprise.

Red caught up with Menace at the next set of double doors, not knowing what was in store for her behind door number two. When Menace pushed open the doors, Red almost lost her mind.

"Are you serious?" she asked as she walked over to the lane, picked up a bowling ball, and then rolled it down the lane.

To Menace's surprise, she rolled a strike.

"Yeah, you got some practicing to do," Red laughed, before putting her finger under his chin to close his mouth.

"You got that," was all he said, before Red skipped out of the bowling room.

She then headed to the second floor, which consisted of a tanning room, a pool room with a pool table that had solid gold pockets, a balcony in the back that overlooked the Olympic-sized swimming pool, a basketball and tennis court, and the grill area. But the master bedroom on the third floor was what really made her fall in love with their new place.

Everything was green and trimmed in gold, Menace's favorite colors. When Menace grabbed the remote off of the nightstand and hit a few buttons, Red watched the 60-inch TV screen ascend from the foot of the bed, the floor-to-ceiling window blinds close, and an old Isley Brother's tune serenade from the surround speakers. Menace walked up behind Red, wrapped his arms around her, and whispered in her ear.

"You ready to break in this California king-sized bed?" he asked as he nibbled on her ear after each word.

Even though he got no verbal response, the moans and grunts said it all. Needless to say, Menace never made it back over to the spot to meet the crew. Instead, he and Red stayed in and made love all through the night.

~ ~ ~

"Where are we on our way to now?" Red asked when Fuzzy entered the city limits of Lucama, the next city north of Wilson.

"To get both of our heads done," she answered as she sat

27

at the second red light and waited for it to turn green, so she could make a left.

Before Red could get a single word out, Fuzzy let her know that everything was on her and she wasn't taking no for an answer. As soon as the light turned green, Fuzzy made a left onto Main Street.

"GU Kutts-N-Styles," Red said out loud when she looked at the letters in big bold print on the salon's front window.

She had heard a lot of talk around town about the salon, but never got the chance to get her hair done at the establishment.

"Ericaaaa!" Fuzzy cheered when they walked into the building.

When Erica looked up and saw her old friend with her arms held open wide, she stopped what she was doing and ran into them.

"Where have you been, girl? I haven't seen you since your wedding," Erica claimed before she took a step back.

"I know, girl. I been busy with the restaurant, and me and Speedy are throwing a grand opening celebration for his new club tomorrow night," Fuzzy admitted. "It's going to be an old-school/throwback jamboree."

"An old-school/throwback jamboree!" Reese shouted from the next room. "You know I'ma be in the place," he sang with his hands in the air, making his usual grand entrance.

"We sure will," Erica added, letting him know that he was not going to anyone's club without her.

Before they could start arguing, Fuzzy interrupted them: "Look, girl, can you do anything with this mess?"

Erica gave Reese one last menacing look and then made her way back over to Fuzzy.

"I got you, girl," she smiled, and then directed her to the empty styling chair.

"Take care of my sis, Reese," Fuzzy said.

Red thought Fuzzy was joking, but she soon found out she was dead serious. Red was glad she let Reese do her hair; and from that moment on, he became her personal stylist.

"I love it," Fuzzy admitted when she looked in the mirror.

Red came from the back looking like a million dollars. After Fuzzy paid Erica and Reese, she handed them both elite VIP passes to get into Club Drama for free. Before the door closed behind them, Fuzzy could hear Erica and Reese start back up. She and Red laughed all the way back to Wilson at how crazy the two were.

~ ~ ~

After dropping Red off at home, Fuzzy called Speedy to check up on him and Sadé.

"Hello, beautiful," he whispered into his phone on the second ring.

"Why are you whispering?" she asked, finding herself doing the same.

"Me and Sadé are playing hide and go seek, and she's it."

Fuzzy shook her head from side to side, just imagining Speedy trying to hide in the most ridiculous places.

"She's going to find you, Speedy. You know that, right?"

"Uh-uh. Not this time. Watch!"

Fuzzy curled her lips to the side. "Speedy, where are you hiding right now?"

"Under her bed," he responded, after making sure the coast was clear.

"Make sure your feet aren't hanging out from up under her bed."

Fuzzy giggled, picturing the sight of Speedy trying to hide under her full-sized bed. Speedy cursed himself when he realized that his feet were indeed sticking out from under her bed, but by then it was too late.

"You're it, Daddy," Fuzzy heard Sadé call out, followed by the sounds of her tiny footsteps running off in the distance.

"See what you made me do?" Speedy blamed as he tried to slide out from his hiding spot. "Shit!" he cursed again when he got stuck halfway.

"See y'all in a few."

"Wait," she heard Speedy call out to her before she ended the call.

When Fuzzy walked into the mansion, she spotted Speedy down the hallway looking into one of the closets.

"I know she's down here somewhere," he claimed, when he looked up and saw Fuzzy headed in his direction.

Before she got a chance to reply, she looked into the white room and saw Sadé's head pop back behind the Italian sectional.

"Did you check the patio?" Fuzzy suggested to buy her daughter a little more time.

"You're right," Speedy agreed, since Sadé loved the outside so much.

As soon as he stepped outside, Sadé ran from her hiding spot and shut the glass door behind him then locked it. Speedy realized that he had been tricked again when he looked back at the mother and daughter duo laughing at him.

"I'ma get y'all!" he promised as he took off toward the

front of the mansion to enter the front door.

By the time he made it inside, the two were in the perfect hiding place. But after searching the mansion for thirty minutes, Speedy gave up.

"Y'all can come out now. I give up!" he called out as he entered his bedroom.

He made his way over to his favorite recliner on the other side of the room and took a seat. As soon as he got comfortable, Sadé eased out from her hiding spot behind the floor-to-ceiling curtain on the left of him, while Fuzzy eased her way from behind the curtain on his right.

"You're no fun!" Fuzzy shouted in his ear, making Speedy hop out of his recliner and reach for his waistline to pull his gun.

Lucky for them, Speedy never carried it on him when Sadé was around.

"I'm sorry," Fuzzy mouthed after realizing her mistake.

"Who wants ice cream?" Speedy shouted, breaking their

awkward moment of silence.

"Meeee!" Sadé cheered and then ran out of the room.

When Speedy heard her little feet taking the steps two at a time, he turned to face his wife. "I'll deal with you later on tonight."

When Fuzzy rolled her eyes and walked passed, Speedy slapped her on her ass.

"Don't make promises that you can't keep!" Fuzzy flirted as she looked over her shoulder and licked her lips, which immediately brought Speedy to an erection.

It never ceased to amaze him that she had that kind of effect on him after all the years they had been together.

"A'ight now!" he warned, then followed her down the stairs, watching her ass jiggle the entire way to the kitchen.

By the time Speedy and Fuzzy made it downstairs into the kitchen, Sadé was waiting in the middle of the floor with her hands on her tiny hips with her head tilted to one side.

"That's your daughter," Speedy whispered into Fuzzy's

ear as he then walked around her to pick up Sadé and carry her over to the island on the far side of the kitchen.

"Thank you, Daddy!" she said, smiling, when he sat her on the tall stool.

Sadé watched patiently as Fuzzy made three bowls of ice cream.

"Don't forget the sprinkles, Mommy!" she reminded, eyes wide open.

Once Fuzzy finished fixing everyone's bowl, she walked over to the kitchen cabinet and grabbed the bottle of sprinkles. Sadé wasted no time when Fuzzy placed the bowls down.

"You want some, Daddy?" Sadé offered, after dressing up the ice cream.

"Yep!" he answered, after turning to Fuzzy and sticking out his tongue at her.

They were always in competition for Sadé's attention. Speedy directed his attention back to Sadé as she made an airplane noise on her way to his mouth. Right before it entered, Sadé lifted up the spoon and ran it straight into the tip of Speedy's nose. Fuzzy tried her best to hold in her laugh, but when Speedy turned to face her, she couldn't hold it in any longer.

"Look, Mommy!" Sadé pointed at the red cherry sticking on the tip of his nose. "Daddy looks like Rudolph the Red-Nosed Reindeer!"

"Oh, that's funny, huh?" Speedy asked as he stuck his spoon in his bowl and flicked it at Fuzzy and then Sadé, which started the ultimate food fight.

Before it was all said and done, Fuzzy and Sadé had won the battle, but he swore to them both that the war had just begun.

3

It was the grand opening of Club Drama, and Speedy was excited.

"How do I look, baby?" Speedy asked once he tied the laces to his brand-new pair of blue and white Lacoste sneakers.

The large alligator logo covered the entire back of his velour blue, white, and yellow sweat suit, which was complimented by a Kangol-style Lacoste hat to match.

"Damn, my man is sexy!" Fuzzy thought to herself, but wouldn't dare boost his already sky-high ego. "You almost look as good as I do," she replied.

Fuzzy then spun around and gave Speedy a full view of her many curves, showing off her red and white Puma sweat suit with shoes to match. Speedy walked up on her and slid on the custom-made dookie rope chain he had had made for her, before putting on his. He wanted to make sure they were going to be the talk of the town for months to come. Fuzzy pranced over to the full-length mirror to make sure everything was intact, before turning to face him.

"How's my ass look?" Fuzzy joked, making her cheeks bounce one after the other.

"A'ight now. Don't make me fuck up nobody at this club!" Speedy warned as he made his way up behind her and pressed his manhood up against her ass.

Fuzzy narrowed her eyes and looked through the mirror at him.

"Don't start with me, Speedy," she reminded him, thinking back to how she had to beat up a chick for being all up in his face the last time they went out to a club together.

Speedy knew what was about to happen, so to avoid an argument, he quickly changed the subject.

"So are you riding with me to the club?" he asked as he moved to her side and grabbed a bottle of Jean Paul and then dabbed a little on his neck and wrist.

"No!" Fuzzy replied as she walked away to the nightstand to get her cell phone.

Speedy knew how the smell of Jean Paul drove Fuzzy crazy, so he walked up behind her and held her in his arms and asked her why not.

"Because I got to go and pick up Red," she answered, before going back to the dresser.

"You know if I don't go get her, she's going to be late."

Speedy walked up behind her again and placed both of her ass cheeks in his hands.

"Stop, baby, before we both be late!" she warned as she closed her eyes, took in a deep breath, and then bit her bottom lip.

He knew he was getting her hot, and he smiled on the inside knowing he could talk his way out of just about any situation he was in with her.

"Make sure you be there on time," Speedy whispered in her ear, before he walked out of the room, leaving her wanting to feel him inside of her. "If you're late, I might just have to spank you when we get back home," he joked, before going downstairs to the front door.

"Is that right? I might just be late on purpose in that case!" Fuzzy shouted back, before grabbing her keys and heading for the stairs as well.

~ ~ ~

The club was packed to capacity as partygoers dressed to impress in their old-school attire. DJ Ollie B had the club going crazy playing old-school hits from rappers like Steady B, 3 X Dope, LL Cool J, Cool C, and Kool G. Rap. What really got them hyped was when he played *Ain't No Half Steppin'* by Big Daddy Kane. Speedy and Menace felt like they were on top of the world as they made it across the dance floor to the tunes of Special Ed's *I Got It Made*, before walking up the steps to get to the section where Lil Man, Lucky, and the rest of the crew were all waiting on them.

As soon as they walked through the door, Lucky

CONNECTED TO THE PLUG 2

staggered over to his mentor and handed him the already lit blunt that he had in his hand. Menace looked around at all of the topless women in the room before taking the blunt and putting it between his lips.

"It's gonna be a long night," he said to himself, before he then took a hard, deep pull of the weed.

Lucky and the crew all burst out in laughter as Menace coughed uncontrollably when the smoke got caught up in his lungs.

"Slow down, big homie. This ain't like that shit we used to smoke on back in the day," Lucky teased, taking the blunt from Menace's lips. "This here is called Smoody. It's $20 a blunt shit," he boasted, before inhaling the weed smoke like a champ.

"Smoody, huh?" Menace repeated, after catching his breath.

No matter what it was called, he knew to take his time with it when he decided to hit it again.

"Yeah, Smoody. This is the best shit around. All it takes is two hits of this, and you'll be right where you need to be for the rest of the night!" Lil Man butted in.

He had one in his hand as well. He looked to his left and handed it to one of the crew members who sat beside him. He was getting head from one of the strippers in the room. Speedy handed Menace a bottle of Cristal and directed him to a booth across the room away from the rest of the crew, where they could look down at the sea of people on the dance floor down low.

"We finally made it!" Speedy held up his bottle of champagne for a toast to them.

Menace held up his bottle with a big smile on his face as he looked around the room. He had always dreamed about what it would feel like to be in the position they were in, and now he knew. "The world is ours!" he cheered.

All the crew members raised their bottles or blunts in the air to toast with the big dawgs before going back to doing whatever it was they were doing before the toast.

Speedy leaned in closer so no one could hear what he had to say next. "Now that you're back, I'm giving you the entire west side of the city. I got spots already up and running, so all you basically have to do is distribute the work, pick up the money, and check on the spots from time to time. That's it! Not more hand-to-hand shit around here. We got crew members for that shit!"

Menace couldn't believe his ears about how easy it was to be a boss. Not being involved in the hand-to-hand thing was going to take a little getting used to, but he was sure he could manage it.

"You ready to do your thang?" Speedy asked in a serious tone.

Menace looked his partner in his eyes and knew they were on a different kind of level. "Have I ever let you down?" Menace replied.

No more words needed to be spoken between the two as

Speedy looked at his watch and noticed that it was almost midnight. After informing the rest of the crew that he and Menace were about to head downstairs, they made their exit.

Speedy and Menace stood with their backs to the bar and stared out at all the people in attendance. They were rocking side to side to the old-school classic *Keep Rising to the Top* by hip hop's pioneer Doug E. Fresh, when two mixed-looking redbones approached them.

"Can I drink with you?" one whispered into Menace's ear, letting her lips brush against it.

Without a second thought, Menace filled her empty champagne flute all the way to the top. She gave him a seductive smile before making a formal introduction to them. "I'm Liz, and this is my sister, Marie," she said, pointing to her sister who stood in front of Speedy and waved her fingers.

Speedy lifted up his bottle of Cristal and offered her a drink.

"I'm not drinking or smoking anything tonight," she

44

declined. "Someone has to have a level head between us,"
Marie joked as she glanced over at Liz, who was too busy
flirting with Menace to even hear what her sister had said.
"You wanna dance?"

Speedy smiled, put his hands in the air, and then shook
his head. "Nah, lil' mama. I don't know how to dance," he
declined.

"Who said you had to? Just stand there looking as fly as
you are, and I'll handle the rest," she shot back, before turning
her back to him and pressing her body on his.

Without notice, Marie dropped down twice and shook her
ass around and around, while coming back up to her feet all
in one swift motion. Speedy looked amazed at how well she
worked her body. His dick instantly became hard as thoughts
of fucking her crossed his mind. The buzz from the blunts and
champagne he and the crew had consumed had Speedy really
feeling himself. He was so caught up in the moment that he
never saw Fuzzy and Red enter the club, until they were right

up on him and Menace.

"Can I speak with you, please?" Fuzzy asked once she tapped him on the shoulder.

Although she seemed calm, Speedy could tell by the look in her eyes that she wasn't asking, she was demanding. Marie sensed Fuzzy's attitude and didn't want to get into the middle of it, so she danced off into the crowd as if nothing was about to happen. Speedy looked over to his partner as Menace tried to explain to Red who the female was who was all up on him.

"Liz, this is my girl, Red. Red, this is Liz," Menace tried to introduce the two, but Red cut him off.

"Bye!" she harshly shouted, getting the attention of a few patrons that stood near the bar area.

Liz sucked her teeth, rolled her eyes, and got ready to give Red a piece of her mind, but before she could, Menace hit her with a head nod that let her know she was dismissed. When Liz was out of earshot, Red let him have it.

"I'll be back in a minute. You good?" Speedy shouted

over the music to get his partner's attention.

Between all the shouting and finger pointing, Menace let Speedy know that he was good. Speedy laughed as he led Fuzzy to the second floor of the club to his private office in the front overlooking the crowd below. As soon as he closed the door behind them, Fuzzy went into a rage.

"What the fuck was that bitch doing all up on you like that, Speedy? You fucking her or something?" Fuzzy was so heated that her face became as red as a cherry bomb that was about to explode at any given moment. She bit down on her bottom lip to control her anger as tears formed in the corners of her eyes.

"Come on, baby. You know I would never disrespect you like that," Speedy pleaded. "I don't even know that broad."

His last comment made things even worse.

"Don't know her! You didn't need to know her! Y'all were practically fucking out there," she shouted, pointing down at the bar area.

47

Fuzzy rolled her eyes at Speedy and walked to the one-way mirror and scanned through the sea of people until she found who she was looking for.

"What do you see in her that you don't see in me?" she asked, with tears rolling down her cheeks.

Guilt immediately overcame Speedy as he walked up behind her and wrapped Fuzzy in his arms, knowing how insecure she had become after their baby.

"Baby, I swear to you it wasn't nothing like that," he replied, while holding her tight. "Don't cry."

Speedy reached up, wiped her eyes, and then kissed the back of her neck. Fuzzy placed her hand on his and then brought it to her lips and kissed it before placing two fingers in her mouth. With his other hand, Speedy unzipped her Puma sweat jacket and exposed her hardened nipples. A soft moan escaped her lips as she began to wind her ass against his erect manhood.

"Fuck me, daddy!" she begged as she placed her hands

against the glass wall.

Speedy slid down her sweat pants to her ankles and then took out his dick.

"Oh, Speedy!" she whined as he inserted inch by inch, until all of him was deep inside of her.

He beat her vigorously for fifteen minutes nonstop. Fuzzy never took her eyes off of the female who was all up on Speedy when she and Red entered the club. She knew the chick would be a problem the way she kept cutting her eyes up at the office they were in, but she planned to nip that in the bud before things got too far. The only thing that cleared her mind momentarily was the gigantic nut when she and Speedy came together. Once they came out of the office bathroom, Fuzzy looked into his eyes. "You better check your bitch before I do," she warned as she headed toward the door.

Speedy knew Fuzzy's words she spoke were true. Even though she seemed nice, sweet, and innocent, Speedy knew she could be as vicious as any soldier he had in his crew. She proved that when she revealed to him that she was the one that put out the hit that killed King, Tawana, and Tawana's baby.

When they made it back downstairs, all hell broke loose. "Go back to the office," Speedy demanded as he began to force his way through the crowd in search of his partner and the crew.

Speedy had a feeling for some strange reason that they were the cause of all the pandemonium in the place, and his thoughts were confirmed when he saw Menace, Lil Man, Lucky, and Tank stomping the shit out of some kid in the middle of the dance floor. By the time he made it over, two big, grizzly-looking bouncers were picking up the guy's bloody body off the floor and carrying him to the exit.

"Yo! What happened?" Speedy wanted to know, once the crew all gathered around him.

They all looked at each other waiting for someone to speak up.

"Come on! Let's talk in the office," Speedy suggested, wanting to get away from the prying eyes around them.

Tank spoke up soon as they were out of earshot of the partygoers. "To be honest with you, big homie, the kid violated you by grabbing all up on Red's ass, and to make matters even worse, when she told the kid who her man was, he was like, 'Who the fuck is he?' Then all of his so-called boys started laughing. That's when I dropped his ass!"

"Good lookin, lil' homie. I would have handled the situation myself if I hadn't gone to the bar for another bottle," Menace thanked Tank, and then gave him a pound to show his appreciation.

Speedy looked over at Red, who was rubbing her right hand as if it was in pain.

"You a'ight?" he asked, when she opened and closed it to make sure it wasn't broken.

"Nigga, please! Ain't nothing soft about me," she joked before turning around. "But this ass."

Everyone burst out into laughter as she dapped Menace. When they made it upstairs to the office, everyone was laughing at how Red stomped the guy out like she was one of the homies.

"What's so funny?" Fuzzy asked, with a confused look on her face.

Red stepped away from the crew and filled in her best friend on what went down when she and Speedy left the bar area.

"Does anyone know who the kid was?" Speedy asked with concern, once he got the crew in a huddle.

He always wanted to know who he or his crew had potential beef with, so he was on point at all times.

"The clown-ass nigga's name was K-Rock," Tank answered.

By the look on everyone else's face, he knew they had no idea who the kid was, so he went into a little deeper detail on the young hustler.

"He's the younger brother of the nigga who took over the north side once King was killed. I think his name is J-something," Tank tried to remember. "J.B. That's it!"

The name instantly rang a bell in Speedy's and Menace's heads as Menace spoke up: "You talking about the same nigga J.B. who used to drive the old beat-up Toyota Corolla back in the day?" he questioned, remembering the shootout he had at Finch Street Park after he sold J.B. four and a half ounces of work that killed his little brother, Tommy. "I thought that nigga skipped town after he got word that I was going to kill him."

Menace couldn't believe J.B. was right under his nose all the time. Speedy saw the look in Menace's eyes and walked to the office closet and came back with an army fatigue duffel bag filled with all sorts of guns and explosives. After issuing them to the crew, he gave strict instructions for everyone to stay on their p's and q's at all times. Even though he knew J.B. was soft and weak, he also knew that with the goons King had hacking him now behind J.B., that would make the scariest nigga have heart. Menace knew that fact as well, so he knew he had to put a precise plan together to seek revenge for Tommy, and that's exactly what he was going to do. After Menace had gotten caught slipping that night outside of his own apartment, he tucked a P89 Ruger in the small of his back and vowed never to get caught slipping again.

"Y'all ready to bounce?" Speedy asked while looking at Fuzzy and Red.

After answering, Fuzzy handed over her car keys to Red and informed her that she was riding home with Speedy.

"I'll be over tomorrow around noon to pick it up," she let Red know, before she kissed her on each side of her cheeks.

"I'm sorry for ruining your grand opening," Menace apologized as they walked out in front of the crew.

Speedy brushed it off as he pulled out his keys and hit the remote to his car, disarming the alarm. The engine came to life when he hit the automatic start button, before he then handed them to Fuzzy.

"Oh, I can drive the bat mobile?" she teased as she snatched the keys from his hand before he changed his mind.

Before he could say anything, Fuzzy was at the driver's side lifting the door to the white-on-white coupe. Speedy shook his head and laughed, before he then turned to address his partner. "Don't sweat it, homie. I would've done the same thing if the shoe was on the other foot," he assured him, and then showed him some love.

After their short embrace, Menace looked around for Red. He almost panicked, until he saw her behind the wheel of Fuzzy's four-door Maybach parked behind Speedy's matching coupe. He watched the glow from the moonlight shine through the panoramic roof off of the diamonds on the side of her D&G glasses.

"Tomorrow I want to introduce you to someone," Speedy announced to get Menace's attention. "I'll be by to get you around noon when I bring Fuzzy to pick up her car."

"I'll be waiting," Menace replied before they parted ways.

When Speedy got into the passenger seat of his coupe, he leaned over and gave Fuzzy a kiss. "To the bat cave, Robin," he joked as he found her favorite singer in the iPod list and hit play. He then reclined his seat all the way back and let the soothing sounds of Mary J. put his mind at ease. They rode for thirty minutes before Fuzzy turned onto their block. She became paranoid when she noticed the same headlights from earlier make the same turn as she did.

"I think someone is following us," she said nervously as they approached their home.

"Pull into the driveway," Speedy ordered as he reached for his strap.

Before stepping out of his vehicle, Speedy put one in the chamber and then lifted his door to step out. Fuzzy's heart dropped as she watched the passenger side window of the car that was following them come down slowly.

"You good, big homie?" Lil Man yelled out, once he

leaned up in the passenger seat.

Speedy gave him a salute before Lil Man threw up the peace sign and told the driver to head to the Ramada Inn off of Highway 264. Fuzzy was relieved as she made her way out of the car and into the house.

~ ~ ~

Speedy was sitting up in bed in deep thought when Fuzzy emerged from the bathroom.

"What's on your mind, baby?" she asked as she crawled in bed behind him and began massaging his shoulders.

"Nothing!" he lied as he craned his neck back to kiss her on the lips.

He didn't want to worry her. But he knew beating up J.B.'s little brother wasn't a good move, and one that more than likely had started a brand-new beef he really wasn't looking forward to having. The only option he had now was to go to the source of things and kill the problem before it spread, which meant drawing first blood.

Slim

Slim stood to his feet with his two bodyguards by this side, and then waved over Speedy and Menace. They had decided to come a little early so Slim wouldn't be waiting on them to arrive, but Slim always showed up an hour early to check out his surroundings. He didn't want to end up like his older brother. Even though he treated Speedy like a son, he had learned in the game to always keep an eye on everyone in his circle, even family.

"So this is the infamous Menace?" he asked as they walked toward his booth.

As usual, Big Mama's Kitchen was deserted, just like the other times he met with Slim there. When Speedy made it to the table, he shook Slim's hand.

"Nice of you to see us," Speedy said, after their short embrace. "As you know, this is Menace," he pointed behind him to his best friend/partner and took a step back for Menace to walk up to shake Slim's hand.

"It's cool," he said in almost a whisper, waving his bodyguards back to let Menace through.

"Any friend of Speedy's is a friend of mine," Slim assured them.

Menace looked at the two bodyguards and then back at Slim. He felt like he was playing the scene of a Godfather movie. He had always heard of connected men, but he had never met one in person.

"I've heard a lot about you," Slim spoke up, interrupting Menace's thoughts.

"Please, have a seat." Slim gestured for them to join him in the booth so they could talk.

"And what have you heard?" Menace asked, looking at his partner.

"Let's just say that I'm impressed with what Speedy has told me about you, as well as from what I've heard in the streets."

Although Slim was only seen when he wanted to be seen, he knew everything that went on in his city.

"We're glad to have you back with us," he admitted, pouring himself a glass of wine and then offering some to Speedy and Menace. They declined his offer, and Slim continued: "As you know, when you left, your crew was only four members." Slim held up his four fingers, counting each one down. "And now there are hundreds of you. I guess now that you're back, Speedy will take me up on my offer. Since he claims the only reason he declined the first three offers was because he needed to talk with you first, since y'all are partners. I must say, Speedy is really loyal to you to decline such an offer."

Menace looked over to his partner proudly and nodded in approval.

"This here that I'm offering the both of you is a whole other level of the game. I'm talking about heroin."

Menace thought about it for a minute before looking at

Speedy. They had dibbled and dabbled in the dope game here and there when they were younger, but the level Slim was talking about would set them straight for life.

"I'm willing to front y'all anything y'all want," Slim informed them.

Speedy wanted to start off somewhat small, so he only asked for one kilo of the black tar. Even though that was a very small amount, Slim agreed to it just to get their feet wet.

"Let me speak to Speedy in private," Slim demanded, excusing Menace from the table. After Menace was out of earshot, he started: "I really like your partner, Nephew. He seems to have just as much respect and loyalty for you as you have for him. That's good! You need that in this game."

Speedy nodded his head up and down as Slim dropped jewels on him.

"But don't let your love for your friend get in the way of business. That can ruin you," Slim warned.

Speedy understood where Slim was coming from and

always respected him for being upfront with him at all times, no matter the situation. He had become more of a father figure to Speedy since he and Fuzzy got together.

"I trust him with my life," Speedy said with pride.

"Very well then."

Slim reached under the table and pulled out a Louis Vuitton briefcase.

"I know we agreed on one kilo, but here are five," Slim said. Before Speedy could protest, Slim cut him off with further instructions. "I'm giving you and Menace two apiece. I want you to give the extra one to Menace as a welcome home gift from me."

Speedy took the briefcase from off the table and then stood to his feet preparing to leave.

"Oh yeah, before I forget: The city is mine," Slim laughed, before sitting back down.

Speedy smiled as he thought back to when he told Menace that the city was theirs now that they had reached the top. That was when he knew Slim wasn't lying when he told him that he had ears everywhere.

When Speedy stepped out of the restaurant, he walked over to a late-model Jetta, handed the briefcase to the female in the passenger seat, and then walked to his coupe.

"So we good?" Menace asked once Speedy hit the start button and brought the engine to life.

Speedy heard the question, but his mind was in a totally different place.

"We're gonna need a bigger crew," he said out loud as he put the Maybach coupe in drive.

He let the mule driving the Jetta get three cars ahead of traffic before pulling out in traffic behind them.

~ ~ ~

A few months passed, and everything was going just as Speedy and Menace had planned. Things were going so well that they decided to take Fuzzy and Red to Atlantic City with them to see an old friend of theirs and do a little gambling.

Once they got themselves settled in at Trump Palace, Speedy and Menace went down to the casino to have a little fun, while Fuzzy and Red treated themselves to a day of pampering at the beauty salon, nail shop, and spa. They spent the rest of the day with an all-out shopping spree in Atlantic City's finest boutiques.

"Yo! That nigga Jay is gonna be shocked as hell when we walk up into the 40/40 tonight," Menace said excitedly as they walked from the cashier's window with $50,000 worth of chips to blow at the craps table.

It had been years since they had taken the trip up to Brooklyn to check up on him. They had come up since then and couldn't wait to show off their status to him.

"I know, right? Especially when he sees Fuzzy and Red by our sides looking like they strolled right off the runway," Speedy boasted as they approached the table. "Let me get $500 on the hard six, and another five on the hard eight," he called out to the croupier.

He then threw down $1,000 and called out to the croupier, and then threw down $1,000 worth of chips in front of him.

"So, what time are we going to check out the joint?" Menace asked as the croupier slid the dice to the roller at the other end of the table.

"I'm not for sure yet, but you know we probably got to get there early to make sure we're able to get in. I heard it be so packed sometimes that they have to stop letting people in. You feel me?"

Menace nodded his head in understanding as the guy rolled the dice down the table.

"You're point is nine," the croupier called out to the roller once he added the numbers up on the dice, and then slid them back to him so he could roll them again.

"Six," the croupier called out after the second roll. "We have a winner on the hard six," he announced as he pointed at Speedy with a smile on his face.

Once Menace saw Speedy's luck, he also put down on the

hard six and eight, and an hour later they both were sitting on over $250,000 apiece. Once the croupier was changed, Speedy and Menace decided to change their luck to the blackjack table.

Menace wasn't doing as well at the blackjack table, but Speedy was winning a little over $75,000 when his cell phone began to ring.

"What's up, baby?" he answered when he heard Fuzzy's sweet voice on the other end.

"Excuse me, sir. Cell phones are not allowed at the table," the dealer warned as he stopped dealing the cards.

"Okay. We'll be up in thirty minutes," he told Fuzzy, totally ignoring the dealer. "Hit me," Speedy demanded, and the dealer flipped the card from the deck.

"Blackjack," he called out. "We have a winner."

The dealer slid Speedy fifteen $1,000 chips, and then looked at Menace to see what he wanted to do.

"I'll stay," Menace announced with a jack of spades and

a king of diamonds in front of him.

The dealer had an ace of clubs facing up, and then turned up the card that was facing down. When he flipped up the eight of hearts, he slammed his fist on the table as his face turned plumb red.

"Let me get my money," Menace laughed as the dealer slid him his winnings.

As soon as the dealer paid out the $30,000 in chips that he owed Menace, he was relieved for the night, and more than likely, forever. When they noticed their luck had changed with the new dealer, they decided to call it a night, so they headed upstairs to their rooms to get dressed for the club.

~ ~ ~

"Girl, I'm so excited," Red squealed to Fuzzy as the stretch Hummer pulled up in front of the 40/40.

"So am I," Fuzzy agreed, digging into her handbag and pulling out her compact to make sure her makeup was intact.

Speedy and Menace watched as the girls put on their

finishing touches before they made their exit. They all felt like superstars as the chauffer walked around and opened the door for them.

Paparazzi were everywhere with their microphones and cameras flashing from every direction. They could hear people standing around in line and asking who they were as they made their way down the red carpet to the main entrance of the door. After whispering a few words into the bouncer's ear, the bouncer lifted the rope, handed them all VIP passes, and then let them enter.

Speedy led the way inside the club and up the stairs to their VIP section, where a bottle of chilled Ace of Spades sat in the center of their table with a dozen roses.

"Now this is the life," Menace claimed as he took his seat and immediately popped open the bottle.

"Heyyyyyy!" Red cheered in her usual hood-rat tone and slid in beside her man.

Speedy and Fuzzy shook their heads and laughed at how

ratchet their best friends could be at times.

"Girl, you know you can't—!" Fuzzy began to protest when Menace began to pour her a drink.

"She can't what?" Menace asked, looking from Fuzzy to Red for an explanation.

After getting no answer from them, he turned to face his partner.

"Don't look at me," Speedy shrugged his shoulders, completely in the blind as well.

Trying to think of the right words to say, Red placed her wine flute back on the table and lowered her eyes. "Menace, I'm pregnant," Red admitted, while playing with her fingers.

She waited a few seconds for Menace to flip the script for not telling him that she had stopped taking her pills.

"I'm going to be a daddy!" Menace shouted out in joy.

Red lifted her head and looked at him in surprise. Before she got the chance to say a word, a waitress entered the room with a message. "Mr. Carter sent me to bring you all to his private VIP room to join him in a toast," she informed with a smile.

Once everyone stood up, they followed the waitress down the hall and up another flight of stairs to another part of the club. The private VIP section was completely different than the VIP room from which they just left. It was like another club in itself. They could tell the partygoers in this part of the club were on a whole other level than those who first entered. Everyone there was dressed in top-of-the-line designers like Vera Wang, Versace, and Louis Vuitton, and many of the patrons were from overseas.

"Do you think B is here?" Fuzzy whispered to Speedy as they made their way to Jay's booth.

"I don't know. I guess we'll find out soon enough," he replied when they stopped at a booth.

From the slant of his fitted Yankees cap, Speedy and Menace knew that it was Jay. Fuzzy and Red were somewhat disappointed once Jay told them B was in Paris on tour and wouldn't be back until Monday morning, but when he gave them tickets to her show the following week at the RBC Center in Raleigh, their faces lit up like it was Christmas.

Fuzzy and Red hit the dance floor while Speedy, Menace, and Jay reminisced about when they use to go up to Brooklyn to see Speedy's uncle Freddie, before he got locked up for bodying an agent on an undercover sting. Jay respected him for not rolling over, even after receiving life plus twenty-five years. They didn't realize how late it had gotten until Fuzzy and Red came back to the booth out of breath and exhausted from dancing all night. After Speedy and Menace promised to come back and check on Jay soon, they called it a night and headed back to their rooms.

~ ~ ~

After Menace dicked Red down and put her to sleep, he went downstairs to the casino area for a drink, and, of course, to try his luck at the craps table before it was time to get on their flight in a few hours. He was up about $25,000 when he began to feel the effects of the alcohol kick in. He thought he was bugging when he heard the sound of a familiar laugh in the distance behind him, so he turned around to see from whom it was coming. She stood with her back toward him talking on her cell to someone.

"Where do I know her from?" he asked himself before addressing the croupier.

"Bets off!"

He quickly gathered up all of his winnings when he saw her heading toward the exit. He made a dash for the door once he placed his chips in his pocket in an attempt to stop the stranger.

"You all right?" Speedy asked as he walked through the door almost knocking over Menace.

He too had snuck out to the casino, after putting Fuzzy to sleep, to try his hand one last time before he headed back to North Carolina.

"Yeah, I'm good, homie. I just thought I saw an old

friend," he replied. *But where do I know her from?* he thought to himself as he followed Speedy to the craps table.

Menace looked back at the exit door one last time hoping the mystery woman would reappear, but she never did.

"Let me find out you had too much to drink and your mind is playing tricks on you," Speedy joked as he placed his bet.

"Yeah, you're probably right," Menace brushed it off and then placed his bet as well.

~ ~ ~

The first thing Speedy and Menace did after they dropped off Fuzzy and Red at the beauty salon was go by Tank's trap house, where they were sure to find Lil Man and Lucky.

"So, how did business go while we was gone?" Speedy asked the crew as they sat on the porch in the cypher smoking on another batch of Smoody.

"Everything went as smooth as a baby's ass," Lil Man answered, once he exhaled a thick cloud of smoke into the air.

"So how was the trip?" Tank asked as he accepted the

blunt from Lil Man.

He took two small tokes as he waited to hear the details of their get-away. Being that he had never been out of the state before, Tank was like a kid at the amusement park anticipating the story. He made a vow that if his chips were stacked up right, he was going to take a trip somewhere real soon.

"It was straight, lil' homie," Menace answered. "We chilled with the homie Jay at the 40/40 after we raped the blackjack and craps table," he boasted.

Speedy and Menace broke down their mini vacation to the crew, and then promised that they all would take off on a real vacation in the near future, before they called it a night.

~ ~ ~

"You sure you don't wanna come in and get yo' ass whipped in a game of pool?" Menace asked, once he stepped out of the car.

The last two times they played, Menace lucked up and

beat Speedy out of a few grand because he scratched on the eight ball.

"I'ma let you enjoy your shoe money," Speedy laughed as Menace took a step back and looked down at his feet.

"Oh, you noticed them?" Menace bragged while rubbing his chin.

"Huh," Speedy grunted. "I had no choice. You reminded me the entire time we were in Atlantic City."

"That's right. I did, didn't I?"

Menace turned soldier style on his heels, and then headed to the front door of his estate.

"The world is mine," Speedy heard Menace yell out, before the windows to his bulletproof Benz rolled up.

When Menace made it into the mansion, Speedy pulled out his cell phone, strolled down to the name "Wifey," and then connected the call.

"Hello, daddy," he heard a mini version of Fuzzy answer the call.

"Hi, princess. Where's Mommy at?"

"She's taking a nap. Want me to wake her, Daddy?"

"No, no, no!" Speedy quickly answered. "I'll be there in a few minutes."

He didn't want Sadé to wake Fuzzy because he had a plan in store for her.

"Go to your room and play with the new toys Mommy brought back from our trip for you," Speedy ordered before ending the call.

Speedy walked into the house ten minutes later. After checking on Sadé, he headed down the hall into his bedroom, where he found Fuzzy laid out across their bed still knocked out cold.

"Hey, baby," he bent down and whispered in her ear, waking her from her peaceful slumber.

"Hey, bae. How long you been home?" she replied with a smile on her face.

Him being the first thing she saw when she opened her

eyes always made her happy. The only thing that could top that was seeing Sadé.

"I just got here," Speedy answered as he walked to the foot of the bed and took a seat.

"What you doing?" Fuzzy sat up on her knees and crawled to the foot of the bed and looked over Speedy's shoulders. "Give me a piece," she pouted.

Speedy sucked his teeth and tried to stand to his feet, but Fuzzy grabbed his arm and pulled him back down. After winning the tussle, Fuzzy snatched the candy bar and took a big bite. After Speedy shook his head and brushed the wrinkles out of his shirt, he headed into the bathroom and locked the door behind him.

"Five, four, three, two, one!" Speedy counted down, and just like clockwork, Fuzzy was banging on the door and trying to come in.

"Hurry up, Speedy, let me in!" Fuzzy shouted.

"I'm using the bathroom," Speedy claimed with his ear to

the door.

He made the mistake of giggling too loud, and Fuzzy realized that she had just been tricked.

"You're gonna pay for this!" she promised, before taking off out of their room with lightning-fast speed to use the bathroom down the hall. "Watch out!" she shouted when she brushed by Sadé on her way down the hall.

Speedy waited for a minute or two to make sure the coast was clear before he made his exit. When he stuck his head out of the door, he cursed out loud.

"Damn!"

Sadé was eating the last little bit of the candy bar that Fuzzy had sitting at the foot of their bed, when her stomach started acting up.

"Daddy, my tummy hurts," Sadé whined, holding her belly.

All Speedy could do was laugh on the inside at his little princess. Speedy stepped to the side so Sadé could go handle her business. When he closed the door behind him, a cold chill ran up and down his spine.

"If its war you want, it's war you'll get," Fuzzy promised.

Speedy turned around and watched Fuzzy's naked body walk over to the dresser to get a set of under clothes, since she didn't make it to the bathroom in time. By the look on her face, Speedy knew she was serious.

Damn! I got to stay on top of my shit now, he thought to himself as he made his way over to his favorite recliner to take a seat. "It's all good in love and war," he stated, making Fuzzy turn and look in his direction.

Even though she was mad, she couldn't stop the smile that had formed on her face that turned into a full-blown laugh when Speedy blew her a kiss. They both directed their attention to the bathroom door when it swung open and hit the wall.

"We'll see who's going to get the last laugh now," Fuzzy joked as they watched Sadé walk out of their room.

She stared at her daddy with menacing eyes the entire time. When she turned to walk out, Speedy couldn't do anything but laugh. Sadé had a boo-boo print covering the whole backside of her pants.

"You really did it now," Fuzzy said, trying to catch her breath.

Speedy knew that he had to be on point at all times now that he had two females at his neck. He just hoped and prayed that they didn't get him while he was asleep.

5

Weeks had passed since Speedy and Menace took Fuzzy and Red out to Atlantic City for the weekend, and Menace still couldn't manage to get the female from the casino out of his mind. He thought about her so much that Speedy began to notice a change in his partner's movements, so once Menace entered the spot, he decided to address him on it.

"What's been up with you, homie? You wanna talk about it?"

Menace knew he couldn't keep what was bugging him away from his best friend for long, so he figured now was a better time than ever to get it off of his chest.

"I saw her, Speedy. She was at the casino," Menace began.

"Who was at the casino?" he wondered as they both took a seat.

"The girl I keep dreaming about. You know, the one that stole my money."

"You talking about Crystal?" Speedy asked in disbelief. "What would she be doing all the way in Atlantic City?"

Menace had asked himself the same question a thousand times and still came up blank.

"Man, you trippin'," Speedy claimed as he then sat back and lit the blunt he picked up out of the ashtray.

"Homie, I'm telling you it was her." Menace gazed off in the distance for a while before speaking again. "You wanna know the crazy thing about it all?" he asked, but didn't wait for Speedy to answer. "Killing her didn't even cross my mind," he admitted.

Menace didn't know why, but for some strange reason he still felt love for Crystal.

"The only thing I want to know is why did she just up and leave the way she did? I know I probably did some fucked up shit in our relationship, but that still doesn't give her the right to take from me."

Menace was on the verge of tearing up when Speedy passed the blunt to him. Their conversation was interrupted by the ringing of Menace's cell phone.

"Yo!" he answered, and then told the caller he would be there in thirty minutes.

As soon as he ended the call, he went into the kitchen, took out the dope and the scale, and then weighed out nine ounces of coke.

"Hit you up later," Menace told his partner as he walked through the living room to the front door.

"You want me to ride with you?" Speedy asked as he stood to his feet.

"Nah, I'm good. I need some time to myself to figure things out," Menace answered, before walking out the door.

Once Menace completed his run, he cruised through the city streets as old memories clouded his head. He was just about to call it a night, when his cell phone began to ring. He ended the call without answering, when he saw that the caller's number was blocked. After hanging up back to back, Menace decided to answer the call to see who it was.

"Who dis?" he screamed into the receiver.

He placed the phone in front of his face to make sure the call wasn't disconnected. When he saw that it wasn't, he asked the question again. Just when he was about to end the call and turn his phone off, he heard a soft female voice.

"I'm sorry, Menace," the caller said, followed by another moment of silence.

Menace's heart dropped as he remembered the voice. He tried to respond but couldn't. He had waited for that day ever since he was released from rehab, but now he was at a loss for words.

"Where are you?" he managed to say through gritted teeth. "Better yet. Were you in—?"

"Yes, that was me in Atlantic City," Crystal confirmed his suspicions.

"Why did you leave?" he asked, getting straight to the point.

"I'm going to be in Raleigh this weekend, and I'll explain everything to you then."

After giving him the time and the place, Crystal ended the call. Now all Menace had to do was figure out a way to get away from Speedy and the crew without drawing any suspicion.

~ ~ ~

Menace sat in the back booth at Bahama Breeze sipping on a glass of Hennessy on the rocks as he waited on Crystal to arrive. He couldn't lie. He was more nervous than ever. Butterflies filled his stomach with mixed emotions at the same time. All Menace knew was that he was there to get some closure on that chapter of his life. There were so many unanswered questions to which he needed the answers, and only Crystal could give them to him.

He stood to his feet as Crystal walked in the building with

a Dolce & Gabbana handbag over her shoulder and her cell phone in her hand. Menace watched as she stopped at the podium, said a few words to the hostess, and then flagged her over when she pointed Crystal in his direction. He hated to admit it, but she was looking more beautiful than he ever remembered as she made her way to the booth in front of him. No words could explain the tears of guilt that began to flow down her face as she leaned in, wrapped her arms around his body, and laid her head on his chest.

"I'm so sorry, Menace. Please forgive me? I—!"

"Shhh," Menace silenced her as he backed up to arm's length and held both of her hands in his. Neither one of them said a word as they stared into each other's eyes and explored one another's souls. Thirty minutes later they were at Crystal's hotel room releasing all of their pent-up emotions. When they finally finished, Crystal explained her reasons for leaving. She then told him about how they met and her holding him down, all the way up to him getting shot outside of their apartment door. Menace felt like he was reading a Donald Goines book as she talked.

"I still have half of the money you had in the safe if you want it," she offered, after telling him about that part of their life.

Menace declined the gesture, and even though he still had love for her, he knew things would never be the same between them again. So he lay there, ran his fingers through her hair, and enjoyed the moment.

"Can we make love one last time?" Crystal asked, knowing that was the end as well.

After putting her to sleep, Menace watched Crystal sleep for the remainder of the night. Before he turned in, he called Red to let her know that he wouldn't be coming home until the morning. He then dozed off as well.

The next morning Crystal caught her flight back to New Jersey, and Menace made his way back home to Red. When he walked into the kitchen, he stood at the door and watched her prepare breakfast. She was dressed in a pair of Menace's Polo boxers and a cut-off halter top that exposed the bottom half of her breasts. He watched as her ass giggled with each move she made.

"Is everything okay?" she asked, once she finished setting the table.

She didn't even have to turn around to know Menace was in the room. When she turned around and saw the stress lines in his forehead, she became worried and walked up in front of him.

"Yeah, everything's good!" he lied as she placed both of her hands on each side of his face. "Did you miss me?" he put on a fake smile to ease her mind, because he didn't want her to worry, especially since she was carrying their child.

"You know I did," she answered as a smile appeared on her face, which was followed by a kiss to his lips.

"Oh yeah? How much?" he asked as he then wrapped his arms around her and grabbed her ass.

"This much!" Red stepped out of his grasp and lifted her halter top over her head and exposed her breasts.

Menace looked at her erect nipples and licked his lips. He couldn't wait to put one of them in his mouth, but before he could, Red took a step back further and hopped on the kitchen counter. She opened her legs, and with her pointer finger, she summoned over Menace before rotating it on her clit. Menace wasted no time in obliging her request and jumped head first into her ocean of love. When he was done, Menace stood up, wiped his mouth with the dishrag, and then headed for the shower.

"You don't want your breakfast?" Red asked as her body jerked on the countertop.

Menace turned back around at the doorway, with a devilish grin on his face. "I'm full," he laughed as he headed back in her direction. "Unless you want some more."

Just the mention of being pleased again made Red's pussy jump, but she waved him off.

"I'm good," she replied as she then hopped to her feet and headed in the other direction.

~ ~ ~

Menace ended the call with Speedy when Red yelled out from the bathroom.

"Bae, you didn't forget that Fuzzy and I are going to get our nails, feet, and hair done today, did you?"

Menace had totally forgotten about their girls' day out, but he wouldn't dare let Red know that. "Nah, I didn't forget," he lied as he went into his pocket and pulled out a stack of money.

"While y'all are out, I'ma need for you to stop by Salena's and pick up my ring for me," he instructed, snapping on his Frank Muller. "The money to pay for it as well as the money to get your feet, nails, and hair done is on the dresser. I also put a little something with it just in case y'all go shopping. You know how y'all do," Menace joked at the girls' shopping habit. "I'm about to go meet up with Speedy. Call me when you're on your way back in."

"I knew you forgot about Fuzzy and my appointment," Red laughed as she entered the room with a towel wrapped around her body.

"What are you talking about? I did remember; the money is right there." Menace pointed to the dresser.

Red shook her head as she walked over to the nightstand beside their bed.

"Oh yeah? Well what is this for?" she asked as she opened the top drawer to pull out the money he gave her the other day to pay for her day out.

"Oh, that? That was the backup money just in case what I left on the dresser wasn't enough," Menace claimed as he turned and headed to the door with a smile on his face.

"Liar!" Red yelled out as she unwrapped the towel from her body and threw it at him, hitting him in the back of his head before he made it out the door.

"A'ight," he warned as he turned around, looked at her

exposed pussy, and then licked his lips.

"You got that one!" Red laughed, before heading to the closet to find an outfit for the day.

~ ~ ~

Menace walked into the spot with a different swagger about himself. He no longer looked as if he was carrying the weight of the world on his shoulders, and Speedy, Lil Man, and Lucky noticed it off the bat.

"What?" Menace asked as they watched him make his way over to the couch to take a seat.

"My nigga must've gotten himself a piece of new pussy last night," Lucky joked, reaching over to give Menace a pound before handing him the blunt he had already lit and in rotation. "So who's the lucky bitch?" he asked once Menace took in the smoke then let it all out, clouding the room up instantly.

Before Menace got the chance to say anything, Lucky's cell began to vibrate, letting him know he had just received a text message.

"Yo, Lil Man! It's those two chicks we booked yesterday at the mall. They want us to swing through and check them out."

Lil Man hit the blunt he was smoking one last time, and then handed it to Speedy before standing to his feet and swiping the ashes from his crisp white tee.

"Well, fellas," Lil Man smiled as he headed toward the door.

"I hate to smoke and run, but duty calls," he laughed and saluted his comrades.

"I want to know about this new chick," Lucky called out, before closing the door behind them.

Once they pulled off, Speedy looked at his partner and waited to hear who this new chick in Menace's life was. It had been a long time since Speedy had seen him so happy.

Reading Speedy's mind, Menace then spoke up. "Who said it had to be a new chick?" Menace put out the blunt in the ashtray and then slouched back on the couch. "Damn! That must've been some of that Smoody shit we had at the club that night!" Menace said out loud as the effects from the weed smoke hit him. He tried desperately to change the subject, but Speedy wasn't having it.

"The girl?" Speedy asked, bringing Menace back to the topic at hand.

Menace glanced over at his partner through slit eyes and then revealed about his secret meeting at Bahama Breeze with Crystal. He even told him about going back to her room, fucking her brains out, and then her telling him about why she left. Speedy was shocked when Menace told him that she even offered to give him back what was left of what she took from his safe. Menace couldn't believe it either, but when she pulled out the duffel bag filled with stacks of $100 bills stacked in the exact way he always put them, the anger of her betrayal quickly subsided. He even told Speedy that he stayed out with her all night until the next morning.

"So what did Red have to say when you came in?"

"Oh, it wasn't nothing. She's cool!"

Speedy looked at Menace like he had lost his mind. He learned firsthand that a woman scorned is the worst kind of woman walking on the face of the earth.

"Oh, she's cool, huh?" Speedy asked with a raised eyebrow.

He then passed Menace the blunt he sat babysitting in his hand. Menace waved his partner off and took the blunt from him.

"Yeah, she even had a nigga breakfast ready for me when I walked through the door and shit, my nigga. Don't hate 'cause you don't got it like dat," Menace joked as he puffed on the blunt twice before he then exhaled.

"Hold up, nigga. You mean to tell me you didn't even fix the food. You're really tripping."

Speedy looked at Menace like he had lost his mind. Menace glanced at his best friend and smiled.

"Wait a minute. You didn't let me finish," Menace stopped him like he had a bright idea all of a sudden. "I walked up behind her as she was setting our plates, right?" he started. "Then she hopped her ass up on top of the counter. I slid her boxers off, and then ate the shit out of her. By the time I was finished, Red was so drained that food was the last thing on her mind."

Menace and Speedy both burst out into laughter at how crazy Menace was for doing that. Menace handed Speedy the last of the blunt, but he quickly declined after listening to the story his homie had just told him.

"What? I brushed my teeth afterward."

"So did you get the closure you needed by meeting with Crystal?" Speedy asked as they walked out of the spot and onto the porch.

"Yep, that was just what I needed."

Hearing Menace say those words was like music to Speedy's ears. Now he was ready to hit the scene full speed, knowing his partner had his head completely back in the game. Things were just about to get turned all the way up.

~ ~ ~

"I thought I told you to call me before you came back home, so I could meet you here," Menace called out to Red, when he entered their bedroom.

"I was, but I wanted to surprise you. I guess that's out of the question now," she pouted as she climbed out of the bath tub, wrapped a towel around her body, and then walked to the sink.

"Did you remember to stop by Salena's to pick up my ring for me?"

"Yes, bae," she responded, popping her lips. "Your cousin, Salena, told me to tell you that you better not forget about the family reunion next week," Red relayed as she pulled her hair back in a tight ponytail. "Oh yeah, and she said just because she owns her own jewelry store, don't think you gonna keep getting no damn discount."

Salena and Menace always joked like that. But truth be told, if it wasn't for Menace, Salena's would not even exist.

"Anyway. Where did you put it?"

"Look on the nightstand beside the clock."

Menace made his way over to the nightstand and picked up the small, neatly-wrapped box. He ripped off the paper and then opened the box before taking out the ring. He held it up to the light and inspected each and every one of the flawless diamonds as he then nodded his head in approval.

"Did it come out like you ordered it?" Red asked as she made her way into the room.

Menace turned around as she modeled her way over to him in a brand-new Victoria's Secret bra and panty set under a matching camisole.

"It's perfect. Just like you," Menace complimented her, before setting it back on the nightstand.

Red made her way over and stood in front of him before pushing him back on the bed. "Sit back and enjoy the show," she demanded as she began to snake her body from side to side.

Menace became hypnotized with each sway of her hips. She took off piece by piece until she was in her birthday suit. When she reached over to get the bottle of lotion off of the nightstand, the sparkle from the diamonds in the ring caught her eyes.

"Oh my God!" she screamed and then picked it up and put it on her finger.

He had completely forgotten about the ring, but he jumped to his feet to see what was the matter. He realized what she was so excited about when she turned around and waved her hand in his face. He watched as her titties bounced up and down, before he got himself together.

"Red, will you marry me?"

Red stopped jumping and looked him in his eyes.

"You know I will marry you," she answered as tears streamed down her face.

She jumped into Menace's arms, wrapped her legs around him, and made him fall to his back on the bed. She then unzipped his jeans. Once she pulled out his dick, she slowly slid down his rod like she was sliding down a sliding board. When Menace didn't come home the night before, Red thought she was losing him, but after the way she sucked and fucked him, she knew he wasn't going anywhere anytime soon. Little did she know that the entire time he was making love to her, he couldn't get his mind off of Crystal. That's when he knew he had a major problem.

~ ~ ~

Lil Man, Lucky, and Tank sat on the porch at the spot having one of their famous ciphers. After taking a long pull from the blunt that was in rotation, Lil Man's mind drifted off into deep thought.

Lil Man was on the way out of the store when he spotted a brown-skinned cutie pull up in front of the gas pump across from his car.

CONNECTED TO THE PLUG 2

"Damn," he cursed as he approached, making a smile come to the cutie's face.

Lil Man watched as she unhooked the nozzle from the pump and opened the gas lid.

"You need some help?" he offered as he made his way through the two pumps to get a better view.

Even though she wore a McDonald's uniform, he could tell she was very curvy.

"Be my guest."

Lil Man walked up and removed the nozzle from her hand and began pumping the gas.

"How much you getting?"

"Ten dollars worth," she replied.

After Lil Man looked the handle, he turned to brown skin and asked for her name.

"Meka," she answered, then asked him his.

"Lil Man."

As they conversed, they forgot all about stopping it at

$10, until the handle unlocked, indicating that the tank was full.

"Oh my God!" Meka whispered, when she saw the gas meter read $45 dollars. Her heart dropped to the pit of her stomach because she only had $20. "Ummm," she began, until Lil Man cut her off.

"I got you, shorty."

Lil Man went into his pocket and pulled out a knot of money and handed her a $50 bill. After going into the store and paying for the gas, Meka came back out and thanked him. She then handed him the $5 that was left over, along with the original $10 she had to pay for the correct amount she wanted. After declining, Lil Man asked Meka for her number.

The following weekend Meka called Lil Man. He thought they were going on a date, but when they met up, Meka tried to give him the $50 that he gave her earlier in the week. Lil Man finally accepted it, after she promised him to go out to dinner and a movie with him. Since then, the two had been inseparable.

"Yo! Pass that shit," Tank called out to Lil Man as he sat with the unlit blunt in his hand.

He had been babysitting it so long that it had gone out. After relighting and putting it back in rotation, Lil Man got up to leave.

"Where you going, cuzo?" Lucky asked, before he inhaled a lung full of smoke.

"To go see my girl," Lil Man responded as he hopped off of the porch and headed to the car.

"Ahhhh," Lucky and Tank waved him off and then burst out into laughter.

6

Speedy and Fuzzy were just on their way home from breakfast at Big Mama's Kitchen when Speedy received a call from Menace.

"We've got a problem!" he informed Speedy when he answered his cell.

"Somebody hit Lucky's spot late last night."

The line went silent, and by the expression on Speedy's face, Fuzzy could tell that the information he had just received must have been bad news.

"Give me an hour, and I'll be right over and make sure everybody's there," he instructed, before he ended the call.

The rest of the ride was in silence. From time to time, Fuzzy would glance over at Speedy, but he remained quiet, not wanting to get in the middle of his business. The first question that popped up in Speedy's mind as he drove to Lucky's trap was who could have enough balls to come on

CONNECTED TO THE PLUG 2

their turf and rob one of their spots. By the time he arrived, his mind was still racing with possibilities. One thing he did know for sure was that the crew was ready to do whatever as everyone stood in the middle of Lucky's front yard strapped from head to toe.

"Is everybody okay?" Speedy asked when he got out of his car and approached the crew.

"Nah, big homie. They pistol-whipped Tank and took all the work and money," Lucky answered, while pacing back and forth across the front yard.

He was ready to go and set it off, and Speedy knew it, but he wanted to let him and the crew know that there was one thing that mattered—and one thing only.

"Fuck the money! What room is Tank in?" he asked, ready to send a few soldiers over to keep an eye on him just in case they tried to send someone over to finish him off.

"He said he wasn't going to no hospital until whoever did that to him was dead," Lil Man answered as he pointed to the door to Lucky's spot.

Speedy couldn't believe his ears. He knew the real reason Tank didn't want to go to the hospital was because he didn't want Speedy or Menace to think he was soft or weak, but Speedy wanted to let him know they would handle the situation only when he went and got his wounds checked out.

After convincing Tank to go to the hospital and get his head stitched up, Speedy put out a $10,000 bounty on anyone involved in the robbery. The fact that anyone had the balls to run up in one of his spots let Speedy know that they had to have a lot of heart; if not that they were completely stupid. Either way he knew he couldn't take them lightly, because both were equally dangerous.

Speedy made his way back home in total silence. The only things that could be heard were the air conditioner blowing and the roaring of the Mickey Thompsons that were on his black-on-black Jeep Rubicon. He only brought out that vehicle when he was on the hunt or, even worse, being hunted. Either way, he was fully protected by the custom-made, bullet-proof automobile. He wasn't 100 percent sure of who was behind such an act on his crew, but he had a slight idea. There was one thing he was sure of, and that was before things were all said and done, the city of Wilson was going to respect his crew or feel their wrath.

~ ~ ~

It took nearly a week for word to get back to the crew that the robbery was payback for stomping out Lil K-Rock at the grand opening of Speedy and Fuzzy's new club a few months ago. It wasn't made clear if K-Rock's older brother, J.B., had anything to do with it, but the beef Menace had with him for just being kin to K-Rock made J.B. affiliated. The bad thing about it was that J.B. didn't even know it yet.

Later on that night, Menace, Lucky, Lil Man, and Tank headed out to the north side of the city to one of J.B.'s well-known trap houses. Menace wanted to send a message to everyone who had something to do with the robbery, or anyone that had any future ideas about trying to step to them, that they better think about it first. That's if they cared anything about their well-being.

"That's the spot right there," Tank pointed as they sat three houses down from the trap spot.

After checking the chambers of their weapons, they all lumped out and raced to the front door. Tank was the first to knock on the door, and once it was opened, he gun-butted the doorman in the head. No sooner did his body crumble to the floor, than the crew bum-rushed into the room where two workers sat playing a game of Madden on a PS3. Tank walked in last after hitting the doorman three more times, and eyed the brown-skinned worker evilly.

"It wasn't me, man. I had nothing to do with it," he pleaded as Tank walked up to him.

But Tank knew he was lying, because he still had blotches of blood on his Timbs.

"Didn't have nothing to do with what?" Tank asked,

before delivering a swift blow across the left side of his face.

The rest of the crew watched as Tank beat the helpless worker to sleep before Lil Man and Lucky headed to other parts of the house and began to ransack it while looking for what they had come there for.

"Jackpot!" Lucky called out once he searched the box of Cheerios.

"Stupid muthafuckas! What black hustlers eat this shit?" he joked as he then emptied two more cereal boxes into a knapsack that sat on the counter.

"Yo! Let's be out," Lil Man shouted out as he walked past the door to the room that Menace and Tank were in, with Lucky right behind him.

Tank looked from Menace to the kid, contemplating on whether to kill him or not.

"Let 'im live, homie," Menace suggested, placing a hand on Tank's shoulder.

Not listening to his better judgment, Tank slowly

backpedaled out of the room without taking his eyes off of the kid. By the time they walked out the front door, Lil Man and Lucky had the car parked out in front waiting for them to jump in.

"What's that smell?" Menace asked once he shut the car door behind him.

Lil Man looked over at Lucky with a wicked smile on his face before he put the car in drive. As he pulled away from the curb, Lucky pulled out a lighter, flicked it twice before staring at its flame, and then tossed it onto the porch of the house. Menace watched as the house was engulfed in flames quickly, before they bent the corner.

~ ~ ~

"I bet them soft-ass niggas are gonna think twice before they try to run up in another one of our spots," Lucky boasted as he gave Lil Man and the rest of the crew some dap.

"I know that's right," Lil Man agreed. "I wish I could've seen the looks on them clowns' faces when they ran out of that burning house."

"If they even made it out," Menace joined as he made his way into the living room from the kitchen with a blunt between his lips.

He blew out a huge cloud of smoke as he looked around the room at all of the loose cannons that surrounded him. Tank sat off in a corner by himself in deep thought until Menace walked over and placed a hand on his shoulder, breaking him from his thoughts.

"What's on your mind, lil' homie?"

"You should have let me kill that clown," Tank answered.

Menace thought the same thing on the way back over to the spot. "Them niggas probably didn't even make it out of the house anyway," Menace tried to lighten up the situation.

"Yeah, you right," Tank agreed, before placing the blunt back in his mouth and taking a long pull.

Just as he was about to speak, he felt his phone vibrate on his hip. He then smiled when he saw a sexy picture of Red on his screen that he took a few nights ago with the word "Wifey" underneath it.

"I'ma get up with y'all sometime tomorrow," he told the crew as he then made his way out the front door.

By the time he reached his car, Menace ended the call and was on his way to home to break in the new California king-sized bed that Red had purchased earlier in the day when she went house shopping with Fuzzy.

When Menace pulled up in his driveway, he decided to call Speedy to update him on what had gone down, so he would be on point just in case anything popped off.

"Y'all did what?" Speedy snapped as he sat up in bed and turned on the lamp that sat on the nightstand, waking Fuzzy from her sleep. "Why didn't you consult with me before you made such a move?"

There was a short silence on the line before Menace finally spoke. "I didn't know I had to get permission to make moves now," Menace replied with a frown on his face.

"I didn't say that, but you at least could have discussed it before you did it," Speedy reasoned.

Menace knew Speedy had a point, but before he could respond, his other line beeped.

"I'ma get at you tomorrow. That's Red beeping in."

Without responding, Speedy just shook his head, ended the call, and then lay back down.

"Is everything alright?" Fuzzy asked, concerned.

"Yeah! Everything's good. Go back to sleep, baby," Speedy answered.

He just hoped the decision Menace had just made didn't cause an unnecessary war that they didn't need at the time.

~ ~ ~

Speedy watched Fuzzy toss and turn in her sleep for the majority of the night, until she woke up in a cold sweat.

"You okay?" he asked, once she woke up with tears in her eyes.

For the past few weeks, Fuzzy had been having

nightmares of the day her father got killed.

"I am now," she answered as he wiped the tears from her cheeks.

Fuzzy placed her head on Speedy's chest and wrapped her arms around him. That was the only place she felt safe and secure at all times.

"You wanna talk about it?" Fuzzy sat silently and listened to Speedy's beating heart as she tried to find the words to say.

"I was eighteen years old when my father was killed. He was speeding on the way to my piano recital when he got pulled," she began reflecting.

The day of Fuzzy's father's death

"Damn!" Wendell cursed, when he noticed the blue lights on the unmarked police car flashing behind him. He knew he was about to receive a speeding ticket since he was going twenty miles over the speed limit. He just hoped he could pay off the officer like he had done so many times in the past.

Once he safely pulled his S600 Benz off the shoulder of the road, he waited patiently for the officer to exit his vehicle. While he waited, Wendell got his registration out of the glove compartment and his license out of his wallet. When he saw the officer who was approaching his car, he knew that he was in for a hell of a day.

"Come on, and make this shit quick," Wendell told Officer Russo, a persistent cop that had it in for him.

"Mr. Biggs," Russo smirked, after reading his custom license plate.

"Mr. Joey Russo," Biggs countered.

This was a game the two always played when they crossed paths.

"Look! I'm really in a rush right now, so if we can skip the chit-chat, I would really appreciate it," Biggs stated calmly.

When he looked up into Officer Russo's beet-red face, he knew he had gotten up under his skin.

"You listen to me, asshole!" Russo whispered through gritted teeth. "You ride around here in your flashy Aston Martin," he pointed out as he took a step back and looked at Biggs's whip, "and live in that big old mansion up on the west side of town," Russo carried on before Biggs interrupted him.

"You meant big-ass mansion on the west side," he corrected, which made Russo's face turn two shades redder.

"You really think you're a real smart ass, don't you? We'll see how smart you really are once your daughter becomes a bastard child," Russo threatened.

That was one game Biggs never played. Not with anyone, especially a cop.

"Let me make myself clear to you. Keep my daughter's name out of your mouth," Biggs warned.

The two stared at each other for a minute until Russo finally put a smile on his face.

"Your days are numbered, Biggs," Russo finalized as he then turned to make his way back to his cruiser.

"Fuckin' pig!" Biggs mumbled under his breath.

He thought that the crooked cop might have heard him when he stopped dead in his footsteps. When Biggs saw him head back toward him, he went into his armrest, took out his loaded .357, and placed it under his lap.

"How old is that pretty little jewel now anyway?" Russo questioned with a wicked grin on his face. "What's her name?" Russo placed his fist under his chin in deep thought. "Chantel, am I right?"

"That's correct. She's doing excellent," Biggs answered, before coming back with a blow of his own.

"How's Alisha and those two beautiful mixed girls y'all have together?"

He knew how to get under Russo's skin and hit him where it hurt the most. The fact that Russo knew Alisha and Biggs had a thing going on before she got with him always got to Russo, mainly because he knew that with a policeman's salary, he could never offer her the things Biggs did. That was the main reason he wanted to lock Biggs up over the years.

"Oh shit!" Biggs cursed as he reached for his .357, but it was too late.

Russo already had his service revolver aimed at Biggs's head.

Bang!

The shot echoed through the air. After looking around to make sure no prying eyes were watching, Russo swiftly made it to his cruiser and peeled out. Unbeknownst to Russo, the homeless man who rested in the abandoned building across the street saw it all, and knew exactly who Mr. Biggs was. After getting in contact with Slim, the homeless man never had to spend another night in a cold abandoned house again.

"It was all my fault!" Fuzzy concluded about her father's death. "If it wasn't for him being in such a rush to make it to my piano recital, he would have never gotten pulled over," she sobbed.

Speedy held her even tighter in his arms, wishing he could absorb all of her pain into his chest.

"It's not your fault, baby!" he comforted. "It was just his time to go."

Even though she knew what Speedy had just said was true, the fact that she had lost her father would always haunt her. Speedy held Fuzzy in his arms all night, until she cried herself to sleep.

7

Two

Two months had passed since Menace and the crew ran up in one of J.B.'s spots, robbed them, took their drugs, and then burned the spot down to the ground. Luckily the one crew member that they left conscious saved the other two from the flames before it was too late. The move Menace and the crew had made without Speedy had him so uptight, but what was done was done. All they could do now was stay on point and be ready for whatever came their way.

Meka, Speedy, and Menace stood courtside and watched as the crew played the biggest game of the summer. They were down by one point, but if they pulled it off, they would be going to the finals for the city championship.

"Push it," Menace yelled once Tank in-bounded the pass to Lucky.

By the time he made it to half court, Lucky had shaken

two contenders and left them on the ground holding their ankles. He then made a behind-the-back pass to Lil Man, who was wide open behind the ark.

"Shoot it, shoot it!" Meka cheered for him to take the winning basket.

Out of his peripheral, he spotted Tank under the goal with a much smaller defender guarding him. Seeing the mismatch, Lil Man shot Tank a no-look pass that hit its target with perfection. As soon as Tank slammed the winning bucket on the guy, shots began to ring out from the side door of an old work van. Bystanders began to scatter like roaches in the projects when the lights come on as they tried to find shelter. Speedy and Menace pulled out their straps and returned fire, while the crew ran to their backpacks to get their guns. It was like World War I as clouds of smoke and pedestrians' screams filled the air. When the van turned the corner, all the gunshots ceased. Speedy looked around for his partner before finding him bent over in the middle of the court.

>22

"Damn!" he cursed as he walked up on his back.

Menace looked up at Speedy with tears in his eyes as he lifted Lucky's bullet-ridden body in his arms and carried him to his Panamera. Once he was in the backseat, Menace jumped in the driver's seat and sped off to the hospital. The streets looked like a parade as they drove through them on the way to Wilson Memorial Hospital in hopes that their homie would pull through.

Once the doctor came out and let the crew know that they weren't able to save Lucky, they rushed out of the emergency room in an uproar. Speedy walked out behind them and tried to calm Menace down, but all Menace saw when he looked down at Lucky was his little brother, Tommy, when he died in front of his eyes.

~ ~ ~

Later on that night

Menace, Lil Man, and Tank rode around the north side of the city all night long in an attempt to find J.B., K-Rock, or anybody they knew who was affiliated with their crew, to wreak havoc on for Lucky's death.

"Yo! I'm hungrier than a fuckin' Somalian with his ribs showing," Tank announced after hearing his stomach growl for the fourth time that night.

Menace looked in his rearview mirror at his young soldier, and for the first time since Lucky was killed, he cracked a smile. "Nigga, yo' big ass stay hungry!" he joked, and then passed back the blunt to Lil Man.

"Where you wanna grab something to eat from?"

Since they were already in the vicinity, he told him to go by the Chinese spot. Menace made a quick U-turn at the corner of Vance and Reid, and then headed for Fikewood Shopping Center. Tank thought he was seeing things when he crossed the light on Highway 301 and pulled into the shopping center's parking lot.

"Ain't that that nigga J.B.'s truck right there?" he questioned, sitting up between the two front seats and pointing in front of the Chinese spot.

Lil Man sat upright in his seat and looked at the tricked-out Yukon Denali.

"Hell yeah! That's that soft-ass nigga," Lil Man confirmed as he pulled out his pistol and put one in the chamber. "Pull up beside it so I can bust that nigga's head," he directed, while reaching for the button to lower his window.

"Nah. We gonna wait for his bitch ass to come out," Menace replied as he pulled up three cars behind his truck.

They didn't realize that he had someone with him until they saw the light from the sun visor come on when they pulled down the mirror. Menace tried to remember where he knew her from, when all of a sudden it hit him.

"That's the bitch that tried to give me some pussy at the

club," he said out loud.

He then wondered if she had been trying to set him up the entire time. That made the situation even worse.

"This nigga's taking too long," he barked as he threw on his mask and hopped out the front seat, with Lil Man and Tank right on his heels.

The sound of the bell alerting that someone had entered the store caught J.B.'s attention, which caused him to pause his conversation on his cell. He almost shit himself as he stared down the barrels of the sawed-off that Menace had aimed in his direction.

"Yo, man! Y'all can have the money," J.B. pleaded as he dropped the phone to the floor and threw his hands over his head.

Tank ran over to the counter and drew down on the cashier and the cook, while Lil Man went to the back to get the tape out of the video recorder.

"Nigga, don't nobody want your fuckin' money," Menace

barked as he walked up in J.B.'s face. "This shit here is personal."

After Lil Man returned with the tape, Menace snatched his mask off. J.B.'s eyes almost popped out of their sockets. "Menace," he said in disbelief.

He had been able to avoid him for so long that he forgot all about the threat Menace had made after his brother's funeral.

"Yo, man, I had nothing to with what happened to you or your little brother after I left the park that day. I swear to you on my mama," he promised as he got down on his knees.

"Is that so?" Menace asked, not convinced. "I guess the next thing you're gonna tell me is that you had nothing to do with my lil' homie Lucky getting killed at the park earlier today neither, huh?"

J.B. looked at Menace like he had no idea what he was talking about. He had heard about the beef his little brother and Menace had, but he told K-Rock to let it go.

"Yo! I'm telling you. Me, my baby mama, and my son just got back in town from Six Flags. I wasn't even around here earlier today when your boy got killed."

Thoughts of Lucky and lil' Tommy flashed through Menace's head. What really hurt him was the fact that after Tommy's funeral, Menace's mother, Ms. Louis, vowed never to speak to him again until he found out who murdered her baby boy and killed them. Right before Menace placed the sawed-off between J.B.'s eyes, he smiled a wicked smile.

"This is for y'all," he looked up and said to Lucky and Little Tommy, before pulling back on the trigger.

As soon as J.B.'s body hit the ground, Menace let off another round into his chest. Menace didn't leave the building until J.B.'s body stopped jerking. As soon as he stepped out of the place, he stared J.B.'s baby mama in her tear-filled eyes. Through all of the commotion, Menace had forgotten all about her in the truck. Breaking eye contact, he walked away and made his way to his car. By the time he closed the door, he heard two gun shots. Menace pulled off shortly after Lil Man and Tank jumped in.

~ ~ ~

Speedy went to Menace's house the following day as soon as he heard the news about the Chinese store massacre. He knew without a shadow of a doubt that Menace and the crew were behind such an act due to the extreme amount of overkill used during the process.

"Yo! What the fuck were you thinking?" Speedy asked as soon as he stepped into the foyer of Menace's home.

He couldn't believe Menace had made such a move again without consulting with him first.

"What do you mean, what was I thinking? The nigga violated the crew when he had his goons run up in the spot and then kill Lucky at the park. On top of that, he was behind Little Tommy getting killed," Menace defended his actions.

"Don't let all this money we're making go to your head and let a nigga catch you slippin', my nigga." Speedy shook his head and stared into his partner's eyes. "You just don't get it, do you?" Speedy asked as he turned and opened the door about ready to leave.

Before he walked out the door, Speedy looked back over his shoulder and asked Menace how much Lucky's funeral was going to cost, and he then dug into his pockets.

"Don't worry about it. It's already been paid for," he informed as Red came downstairs and waved at Speedy.

Speedy acknowledged her with a nod of his head and then headed toward his car.

"Is everything okay?" Red asked once Menace shut the door.

"Things couldn't be better," he replied, before he kissed her on top of her forehead and then headed upstairs to their bedroom to take a nap.

~ ~ ~

"So what's up with you and Menace?" Shelia asked Speedy as she dropped eighteen ounces of coke and baking soda into the Pyrex pot on the stove.

For the last month or so she could feel the tension in the air between the two whenever they came around her. He shook his head in defeat before answering her question.

"Pssss," he let out a deep breath. "Where do you want me to begin?"

"How about the beginning?"

"Auntie, it's like every time things start to go good for us, Menace seems to somehow turn it bad," Speedy explained from his side of the story.

"That's how the game goes sometimes. You just gotta take the bitter with the sweet," Shelia reminded him as she turned the stove on high and watched as the coke turned into gel form.

"Yeah, I know, but you haven't heard the worst part yet."

She looked over her shoulder at Speedy as she lifted the pot off the burner, walked over to the sink, and turned on the cold water.

"He got back up with Crystal," he informed as Shelia let drops of cold water run onto the side and over the edge into the Pyrex pot, making the gel inside it form into a hard white solid.

She couldn't believe her ears as Speedy went on.

"He claimed he needed some closure on that chapter in his life so he could move on, but I tell you, Auntie, I think there's more to it than that."

Shelia made her way over to the table where Speedy sat with a scale, a box of brand-new razors, several zip lock bags, and a plate in front of him.

"So you think she's the reason why Menace has been acting the way he's been acting?" she asked, before emptying the crack from the Pyrex pot onto the plate.

"I don't know," he answered honestly. "But what he needs to realize is that now we're on a totally different level than we were on before he left. Rules are different. They must be respected and followed if we intend on surviving. I'm trying to get him to see that. I just hope I can before it's too late."

Shelia's ex-boyfriend was on the same level Speedy and Menace were on, so she knew exactly where he was coming from; and just like Menace, he too was also a hothead and made moves without thinking of the consequences of his actions. Lucky for him, he got picked up by the feds before the HNIC had a chance to get to him.

"Speedy, I've known the both of you ever since y'all were little snot-nosed kids running around asking for a quarter to get freeze cups from the candy lady at the corner," Shelia joked, lightening up the situation. "Talk to him. I mean, explain the position he's going to put y'all in if he keeps moving the way he's moving. Do that for me," she begged. "Before it's too late."

Speedy looked over at Shelia and saw tears beginning to form in the corner of her eyes.

"I know he'll listen to you. He always has," she

concluded.

Speedy promised to have a serious talk with Menace. He just hoped he could get through to him this time around.

After they finished bagging up the crack for distribution, he headed out to his various spots to hand it out.

~ ~ ~

It was a little after midnight when Speedy walked into the house. Before he went to his bedroom to take a shower, he made a quiet detour to his daughter Sadé's room to check in on her like he did every night when he got home. He could see her resting peacefully from the glow the nightlight gave off as he approached her bedside. She was Speedy's bundle of pride and joy. He and Fuzzy spoiled her to no end with their love and affection. She was two years old and had more clothes and jewels than the average adult. After pulling the comforter up to her neck, Speedy bent down and kissed the top of her head.

"Goodnight, princess," he whispered in her ear, before he

turned and headed toward the door.

"Night, night, Papa," Sadé whispered back, followed by a light giggle.

She always played possum to fool Speedy whenever he would come in and check on her.

"Night, night!" he replied as he blew her a kiss and walked out of her room.

"Your daughter is something else," Speedy declared when he walked into the room where Fuzzy was sitting Indian-style in the middle of the bed going over receipts from the restaurant and the club.

"So she fooled you again," Fuzzy laughed as she slid the papers to the side so Speedy could take a seat in front of her.

"You know I have a weakness for girls with pretty eyes and a big smile," Speedy joked as he took off his shirt and threw it at her.

"Ewww! You stink," she shouted as she caught it and threw it back at him.

CONNECTED TO THE PLUG 2

After dodging the shirt, he made it over to the bed and took a seat with his back facing her.

"So how is Menace taking Lucky's death?" Fuzzy asked with concern, before placing her hands on his shoulders and beginning her massage.

"He's cool," Speedy answered in a dry tone as he closed his eyes and loosened up.

Fuzzy could feel the tension ease away as she worked her magic.

"He's cool? What kind of answer is that?"

Speedy knew she wasn't going to leave it alone until he revealed what happened when he went to see Menace earlier, so he went on and told her everything that had been going on, leaving out the part about getting up with Crystal.

"Baby, put yourself in his shoes. Then ask what you would have done," Fuzzy reasoned, trying to get him to see it from Menace's point of view.

"So you on his side?" Speedy defended, raising up from

his slouched down position.

"Do you have to ask that?" Fuzzy snapped, after pushing him on his back.

"I'm sorry, baby. I don't know why that even came out of my mouth. I just got a lot on my mind. Please forgive me. It's just that I'm trying my best to get Menace to understand that since we're in a higher position in the game, we not only got to *think* smarter, but we got to *move* smarter as well. We got to stay ahead of all the stick-up kids, the snitches, the police, and, most of all, the people around us," Speedy rationalized. "This shit here is chess, not checkers. We're running an organization now, you feel me?"

"I feel you. Do you feel me?" Fuzzy asked as she pressed her erect nipples against his back.

Speedy turned his head and looked back at her, and before he could say anything, she placed her tongue deep into his mouth and grabbed his dick.

"Come on," she demanded, when she removed her tongue

and led him to the bathroom, where she relieved him of the

rest of the stress he had inside.

8

After Menace met up with Speedy to hear what was on his mind, he decided to take a little trip out of town for the weekend to get his mind back on track. Once his plane landed in Philadelphia, Crystal was there to pick him up.

"I see that you took good care of my baby," Menace smiled, placing his luggage in the back of his old mint-green S-Type Jag.

"Yeah, I knew how much it meant to you. I almost thought I was in competition with it when we were together," she admitted as Menace hopped in the passenger seat and closed the door.

"Yeah, right! You know I never put anything or anyone before you," Menace responded truthfully.

Silence filled the air as they stared deep into each other's eyes.

"Come on, move it," the cab driver behind them screamed, making them break eye contact.

Crystal reached down and put the car in drive before jumping on the expressway.

Thirty minutes later, Menace saw a sign in big red letters that read "Trenton Makes and the World Takes" as they crossed the bridge into Trenton, New Jersey. Crystal drove him around and showed him the sights before they went to Atlantic City. They strolled down the boardwalk venturing from store to store, which ended with them lying on the beach and reminiscing about their past together. Before the night was over, they were in the casino's lobby at the blackjack table. Even though Menace had lost a little over $10,000, he had the best time since he got out of the hospital.

The weekend came and went so fast that Menace didn't even realize it until Crystal drove him back to Philadelphia International. He then loaded the plane and headed back to Raleigh-Durham International Airport to get back on his grind.

For the next few months, Menace and Crystal talked daily and once again built up a relationship. When they weren't talking on the phone, Menace managed to sneak away from Red, Speedy, and the rest of the crew, and crept up to Trenton to see her. On one particular weekend that Menace made a getaway, Speedy had him followed.

"Yo!" Speedy answered his cell, when he saw Ben's name pop up on the display screen.

Ben Rothlenburger was a sloppy, short, overweight Jewish man with a receding hair line. The only reason Speedy retained him for his services was because he came highly recommended by Slim. After doing a little research, he found out Ben was one of the most sought-after private investigators in the country. That alone let Speedy know he would be perfect for the job.

"Well, your boy is here in Trenton," he informed as he watched Menace enter into a two-story row house on

Brunswick Avenue.

"Trenton?" Speedy repeated, trying to think of who they knew in Trenton.

No name entered his mind at the time as Ben continued with his report.

"Yep," Ben replied as he looked up at the house and then wrote down the address for Speedy. "The chick he came to see doesn't look bad either. The pussy must be good enough to have your boy take flights out to New Jersey," he laughed, remembering watching the stallion get out of her car with Menace dead on her heels.

"New Jersey," Speedy said under his breath.

"That's what I said. I hope that's not going to be a problem with you paying for my services," Ben wanted to know.

"Oh no. There won't be no problem," Speedy assured him, before he asked for the address.

Ben ran down the address and directions to the house and

then ended the call. Speedy knew exactly who the female was that Menace was visiting in New Jersey, by Ben's description of her. Speedy booked the first available flight to Philadelphia International, and then headed to RDU to catch the plane.

As soon as he landed, Speedy headed to the west end of the airport to the Budget car rental building and picked up the car he had reserved for the day. About thirty minutes later he was exiting off Route 1 onto the Oden Avenue off ramp, and then onto Brunswick Avenue.

"There's 543 . . . 541 . . ." he counted down until he got to 539, which was the address Ben had given him.

As he parked a few cars away, he had no idea what he was going to say to his partner. A little over an hour had past when he noticed Menace's old mint-green S-Type Jag pull up in front of the address. He watched as Crystal and Menace entered the row house, before making his way to the door. After the third knock, Speedy and Crystal stood face-to-face for the first time in over two years.

"Aren't you going to invite me in, sis?" he asked with a smile on his face.

"You have company," she yelled over her shoulder to Menace while rolling her eyes and stepping to the side for Speedy to enter her house.

When he came in, Crystal closed the door behind him. Menace walked into the front room and couldn't believe his eyes when they landed on his best friend in front of him.

"What are you doing here?" he asked with a slight attitude.

"You following me now and shit?"

Crystal walked out of the room so they could have some privacy for the heated argument she was sure was about to occur.

"What am I doing here? I should be asking you the same thing. I thought you said it was over between the two of you," Speedy said in a very calm voice. "Whatever happened to all that closure bullshit you claimed you got when y'all last saw each other?" he continued as he looked into his partner's eyes.

"Fuck you, nigga! I don't gotta explain shit to you. That's your problem now. Always trying to control everyone else's life, when you should be trying to focus on your own shit! So let's get it straight right here and now," Menace barked through gritted teeth and with his fist balled up tight. "You don't run shit over here."

Speedy couldn't believe the words that had come out of Menace's mouth. He had no idea he felt that way, and it really bothered him, because all he ever did, he did it for the both of them.

"So what, you gonna swing on me now?" Speedy asked, taking a step back ready to defend himself. "You know what? I'm through with you," he calmly stated as he nodded his head up and down and then backpedaled to the front door.

He didn't even recognize the stranger that stared him in his eyes. It was like Menace was a totally different person now. After he walked out of Crystal's house, Speedy got in his car, drove to the airport, and then flew back to RDU International Airport.

As soon as his plane touched down, Speedy reached in his pocket and turned on his cell phone. When he looked down at the display screen, he noticed that he had several voice messages from various callers. He listened to them all; however, most of them were from Menace telling Speedy that he needed him to get in touch with him as soon as possible. After deleting them all, Speedy hit the power button on his phone and turned it back off. He didn't want to think about nothing on his ride home beside his pride and joy: Sadé.

~ ~ ~

Fuzzy stood in the doorway of their bedroom with her arms folded across her breasts and a smile on her face as she watched Speedy and their daughter, Sadé, in the middle of their bed taking a nap. She always enjoyed seeing them share their little father and daughter moments together. They always seemed to remind her of her and her father before he died. Speedy spoiled Sadé the same way her father used to spoil her—or maybe more. Those thoughts were short-lived when the ringing of their door bell brought her back to the present as she tiptoed across the room to look at the monitor to see who was at the door.

"Baby," she whispered to Speedy, once she walked over to the bed and tapped his shoulder lightly.

"What's up, baby?" he asked as he lifted up his head to see what she wanted.

"Lil Man and Tank are downstairs at the front door," she announced, once he sat up in bed.

He knew it had to be something important for them to come to his house unannounced, so he got up and answered the door. As soon as he opened it, he knew nothing good could come out of their visit when he saw the tears in their eyes.

"They killed him!" Lil Man sobbed as he broke all the way down.

"They killed who?" Speedy asked, looking from Lil Man to Tank for someone to answer him.

"They killed Menace!" Tank answered, wiping the tear from his eyes.

The news hit Speedy like a ton of bricks to his face. All sorts of questions popped up in his head when he thought about how he didn't bother to return his phone call to see what Menace had wanted earlier, especially when they told him Menace was killed somewhere in New Jersey. Crystal setting Menace up after he left was the first thing that popped in Speedy's head. A part of him blamed himself for not bringing Menace home with him, and if either of their egos wasn't so big, he would have done just that.

"Meet me at the spot in an hour. Make sure the rest of the crew is there as well," Speedy ordered as he walked Lil Man and Tank out of his house.

"Is everything alright?" Fuzzy asked when she came back in the room from putting Sadé in her own bed.

She already knew the answer when she saw the tears in Speedy's eyes when he turned around and looked up at her.

"What happened?"

Without leaving out a single detail, he broke down everything that had happened, even the part about Menace going up to Trenton to see Crystal for the past few months.

"If I just would've called him back, Menace would still be alive."

Fuzzy sat beside him on the bed and held him tight in her arms and rubbed his back.

"Baby, there was nothing you could do," she assured him. "It was just his time to go."

Even though Fuzzy spoke the truth, it hurt knowing that he and his partner were on bad terms when he died. Once Speedy got himself together, he told Fuzzy to call Red and give her the bad news while he headed out to Menace's mother's house to inform her.

"After I leave there, I'm going to the spot to handle the

CONNECTED TO THE PLUG 2

situation."

Fuzzy picked up her cell to call Red as Speedy put on his jacket, retrieved his keys from the dresser, and then walked toward the door.

"I love you, baby," Fuzzy called out as Speedy headed downstairs.

"I love you more," he replied, never breaking his stride until he got to his car.

Fuzzy watched him as he backed out of the driveway, until he was out of sight.

"What's wrong, girl?" Red screamed into the phone, getting Fuzzy's attention.

She had forgotten that she had called Red, and now that she was on the phone, she had no idea how she was going to break the news of Menace's death.

"I'm on my way over," Fuzzy assured her, before hanging up the phone in her ear.

She knew Red was going to need a friend, so she decided

to tell her in person instead of over the phone.

Fuzzy bundled up Sadé in her comforter, got in her car, and thought of the words to say to her best friend.

~ ~ ~

After giving Ms. Louis the money to bury Menace, Speedy met up with Lil Man, Tank, and the crew at the spot. Shelia took the news of Menace's death harder than Speedy had imagined, and she locked herself up in her room. She wouldn't open the door for anyone, not even Speedy. They all sat at the kitchen table as Speedy discussed with the crew how things would be run now that Menace was gone. Once that was done, he sent everyone on their way and put Tank in charge of things, while he and Lil Man went out of town to handle their business.

Speedy and Lil Man sat outside of Crystal's row house and waited for her to arrive. Speedy needed to get down to the bottom of Menace's death. He prayed, for Crystal's sake, that she wasn't behind what had happened to his best friend.

If she was, he was going to make sure she died a painful death. After staking out for several hours, Speedy and Lil Man decided to break in her house and wait inside for her.

It was one o'clock in the morning when they heard the sound of a set of keys fumbling outside the door, followed by a few curse words. Once Crystal found the right key, she stuck it in the lock cylinder, opened the door, and then turned on the light. As soon as the door closed behind her, she looked up and almost lost her breath.

"What the fuck y'all doing in my house?" she questioned, looking from Lil Man to Speedy.

Just as she was about to try her luck and run for the door, Lil Man cocked the hammer back on his .357 and pointed it at her head.

"Don't even think about it, bitch!" he threatened, ready for Speedy to give him the word to end her life.

Crystal saw the look in his eyes and knew he would send shots her way without giving it a second thought, so she walked over to the couch and sat down.

"What happened?" Speedy wanted to know.

Something just didn't seem right to him about the entire situation. Before he left to head to the Philadelphia airport, things seemed to be good between Crystal and Menace. For the life of him, Speedy couldn't figure out what could've possibly gone wrong from the time he left her house to the time his plane had landed back in North Carolina.

Just as Crystal was about to answer him, her front door swung open and drew everyone's attention. Speedy couldn't believe his eyes.

"I thought you were—!"

"Dead," Tawana finished as she walked in.

When the door closed behind her, she made her way over to the couch and sat beside her sister. So many questions ran through Speedy's mind.

"No! You're not having a bad dream," Tawana said sarcastically as she looked at the confused look on Speedy's

CONNECTED TO THE PLUG 2

face.

So many feelings began to resurface as tears welled up in their eyes when they looked at each other.

"Let my sister go, Speedy," Tawana requested. "She had nothing to do with Menace's death. I swear on my son."

"She had nothing to do with Menace's death. I swear on my son." That last statement caught Speedy's attention.

For the past few years, he always wondered if the child Tawana had was his or not.

"Was he my kid?" Speedy wanted to know.

A single tear fell from Tawana's eye, but before she could answer, the front door flew open once again.

"Damn, bae! I thought you said you had to use the bathroom right quick. You must have had to do the number—!" King began to joke, with Tawana's son in his arms, but he cut it short when he saw Speedy and Lil Man with guns in their hands and Tawana and Crystal sitting on the couch in tears.

"Mommy!" the kid cried as King put him down and threw his hands in the air. "What's wrong, Mommy? Why are you crying?" he asked as he ran over to the couch and leapt up onto Tawana's lap.

He wrapped his arms around her neck and began to pat her on the back to console her.

"Mommy's okay, Junior," Tawana replied and held him tight.

Speedy didn't need any confirmation from anyone as to whether or not Junior was his son. Lil Man couldn't believe his eyes as he aimed his gun in King's direction. He was more confused now than ever—and so was Speedy. He had a feeling King was behind Menace's death, but he had to be sure before he put a bullet between his eyes.

"I'm not carrying," King admitted, then lifted up his shirt and did a complete 360 before joining Tawana, Junior, and Crystal on the couch.

"Now what?" Crystal asked with an attitude.

She couldn't believe she was being held hostage in her own house, especially by Speedy and someone she didn't even know. Speedy stood quietly in front of them weighing his options.

"You wouldn't dare be doing shit like this if Menace was still alive," she continued, adding fuel to the already burning flame.

"Man, let me pop this bitch!" Lil Man begged as his trigger finger began to itch.

Speedy held up his right hand, silencing Lil Man and Crystal so he could think clearly. "All I'm here for is to find out what happened to my best friend," Speedy admitted as he began to pace the floor. "After that you'll never hear from me again."

Crystal looked from Tawana to King and then to Speedy. She was about to say something, but King cut her off.

"I killed him!" King confessed, standing to his feet ready to face whatever consequence came with his actions.

155

Tawana handed Junior to Crystal and jumped up in front of him as Speedy pointed his gun toward King's forehead.

"It's okay, Tawana," King assured her and then moved her to his side.

"It's not what you're thinking, Speedy," Crystal defended him.

"Shut the fuck up, bitch!" Speedy pointed in her face. "If it wasn't for you, my partner would still be alive now," he screamed.

"That's your problem now. You don't wanna listen to shit. Well you're gonna listen to me."

Crystal sat Junior on the couch and stood face-to-face with Speedy.

"It's your fault Menace is dead. When you left here, Menace was mad at you."

Those words felt like a slap to Speedy's face.

"That's right," she rubbed it in. "That's when I told him about King and Tawana not being dead and how we all moved up here to stop the beef between you, Menace, and King. King chose to be the bigger man, so he decided to pack up and leave everything behind and raise a kid he knew wasn't his own. That's right, Junior is yours. His real name is also Marcus."

Speedy looked on the couch at Little Marcus, and his heart felt shame.

"But I saw—!"

"You saw King's shot-up Bentley, but it was his bodyguard along with his wife and son in his car, not us," Tawana interrupted. "How could you want me and your son dead?" she asked as tears streamed down her face.

"I didn't," he admitted, then wiped his eyes. "That's neither here nor there now. What I want to know is how Menace got killed up here," he said, bringing his attention back to King.

"It's like this," he began. "I came over here to drop Junior off so Crystal could keep him for the weekend, and when I knocked on the door, Menace opened it. I could tell by the look in his eyes that he wanted to kill, and when he pulled out his pistol, he confirmed my beliefs. He tried to call you several times as he held me at gunpoint with Junior in my arms. When he let me put Junior down, he ran into the back room to get his aunt Crystal. When he watched Junior leave the room, I knew that would be my only opportunity to take the gun from Menace, so I took it, and before you know it, we were tussling on the living room floor for the gun."

Speedy bit down on his bottom lip as he listened to King's side of the story.

"All I remember after that is Crystal standing in the doorway yelling for both of us to stop. That's when the gun went off."

Speedy tried to control his anger, but so many emotions were racing through his head all at once. He wanted to cry, he wanted to kill, he wanted to turn back the hands of time and be there for his son and Tawana; but most of all he wanted

King dead. That's when he sent a slug to the middle of King's forehead, sending him slamming into the wall behind him and then down to the floor.

"Give me my son, bitch!" Speedy screamed at Tawana as he made his way over to the couch and snatched up Junior.

"Please don't, Speedy!" Tawana begged as she pulled and tugged at his arm in an attempt to free their son from his grip. It was no use, because the cold look Speedy gave her made her release her grip and back away. Speedy walked to the car with his son in his arms. After he fastened Junior in the backseat, he heard two shots go off from Lil Man's .357 before he exited Crystal's house and jumped in the passenger seat. On the ride to the airport, Speedy would glance in the rearview mirror at Junior, who was sleeping peacefully.

~ ~ ~

The entire ride from RDU International Airport to Wilson was made in complete silence. The only sound that could be heard were the sounds of the Yokohama tires speeding down the highway and the light whimpers coming from Junior in the backseat. Speedy wanted so badly to ask Lil Man what happened when he walked out and left him to take care of Crystal and Tawana, but every time he glanced in his rearview mirror, he decided that now was not the time. Besides, Lil Man was lost in his own thoughts as he stared out the window at all the passing trees that went by. Speedy figured he was thinking about the loss of his cousin Lucky as well.

"Yo, I'ma holla at you tomorrow," Lil Man saluted his comrade, before he hopped out of the passenger seat and headed to his awaiting Lincoln LS in front of the spot.

He'd had a long night and didn't even bother to go up to the spot and let the crew know they were back. All he wanted to do was go home and get some much-needed rest. Speedy pulled away from the curb and headed home. Now all he had to do was figure out a way to break things to Fuzzy about their new situation.

9

"How did things go?" Fuzzy asked when Speedy entered the bedroom.

She watched as he made his way to the bed where she sat and held his hand out to her. She placed her hand into his and followed as he led the way to Sadé's bedroom. When she looked inside, she didn't have to ask who the little boy was who was playing with their daughter, because the resemblance said it all. She closed the door behind her and then walked back to their room with a thousand questions running through her head.

"Who's the woman?" she asked, when Speedy closed the door behind him.

Fuzzy turned around with tears in her eyes and waited for Speedy to respond. The first person who popped into her mind was the female who was all up in his face the night of the grand opening months ago. She had an idea there was more to the story than was told to her, and by the age the little boy in the other room appeared to be, he and Sadé were around the same age. Just the thought of Speedy being unfaithful to her was making her sick. She held in her stomach in an attempt to keep the contents from coming up.

"It's not what you're thinking," he replied as he wiped the tears from her eyes. "I would never take a chance of losing my family over another woman," he assured her. "That's the son I had by Tawana."

Fuzzy looked at Speedy with a confused look on her face.

"They weren't in King's Bentley when it got shot up," he informed her.

By the look in Fuzzy's eyes, he could tell that the thought of King coming after them had crossed her mind.

"You have nothing to worry about. They're all gone now."

After Speedy explained the reason Junior had to live with them now, Fuzzy believed everything Speedy had revealed to her when he went to New Jersey. When Speedy finished, Fuzzy placed both of her hands on the side of Speedy's face as he put her lips on his. They were interrupted by Sadé and Junior running into the room.

"Mommy, Mommy!" Sadé cheered. "Junior, Brother," she pointed, showing her mother her new brother, who held onto Speedy's pants leg and hid behind him.

Fuzzy smiled and looked down as Junior peeked his head from behind Speedy's leg. She couldn't deny that he was Speedy's son when she looked into his eyes.

"Hi, Junior!" Fuzzy held her hand out to him. "Come here. Let me see you."

Junior slowly and shyly moved from behind his daddy's leg, with his head held to the floor.

"You hungry?" she asked as she put her finger under his chin and lifted up his head.

Junior nodded his head up and down as a smile crept to his face.

"So, what do you want?" she asked, looking from Sadé to Junior.

"Ice cream!" Sadé screamed as she then took off running toward the kitchen.

Fuzzy was about to deny her, until Junior snatched away and headed out of the room behind her.

"I guess ice cream it is." Fuzzy shrugged her shoulders and then headed toward the door to catch up with the two Energizer bunnies.

"Thank you," Speedy said gracefully.

Fuzzy stopped when she reached the door, and then turned around.

"No. Thank you," she replied. "Now that we have the son you've always wanted, I don't have to mess up this perfect shape," Fuzzy teased as she ran her fingers up and down her body.

"Mommy!" Sadé yelled from the kitchen, which interrupted their flirting session.

"Make sure you save some for later. We're gonna need it," Speedy promised, and then licked his lips seductively.

"I know that's right," she agreed before hurrying out of the room and downstairs.

After cleaning up and giving the kids a bath, Fuzzy tucked them into bed.

"I thought you forgot about me," Speedy smiled, when Fuzzy entered their bedroom with her arms behind her back.

"Never that," she replied, only to reveal the half-empty carton of vanilla ice cream behind her back.

She seductively licked her top and bottom lips as she made her way over to their bed. As Fuzzy climbed into bed, Speedy hit the iPod button on the remote and the soft voice of Anita Baker sang through the surround sound system. He wasted no time getting down to business. As he pleased his wife, she made soft moans and took deep breaths. Once her body was covered with ice cream, Speedy licked it all off. By the time they finished making love, they were tired and winded, not to mention sticky. After they took a long, hot shower, they got back into bed, made love again, and were out for the count.

~ ~ ~

Fuzzy was up and out of the mansion first thing in the morning. She wanted to return from shopping for Junior before Speedy and the kids woke up, since Junior had nothing to wear besides the clothes that were on his back. To her surprise, when she entered the house, there was total peace and quiet. She figured the kids had to be asleep still since they had stayed up until the wee hours of the morning playing Sadé's Wii entertainment system. When Fuzzy made it up the stairs, the first place she looked was in Sadé's room, and just like she had figured, they were both laid out on the floor in front of her television with the remote controls to the Wii in their hands. After turning off the game system and the television, Fuzzy crept out of the room and down the hall to the guest room, which she and Speedy had decided to turn into Junior's room. Once she put the clothes in the shopping bags away, she went into her and Speedy's bedroom.

"Speed—!" Fuzzy began to call out, until she saw him balled up under the covers resting peacefully.

A single tear dropped from her eye when she thought to herself, *I can't believe I almost didn't give him a chance.*

Once she took off her outfit, she walked across the room and joined him.

"Thank you," Fuzzy spoke to God before closing her eyes.

"You're welcome," she heard a response.

Speedy knew he had startled Fuzzy by his response.

"Ouch!" He jumped when he felt her pinch his side.

When he turned to face her, Speedy was caught by surprise by Fuzzy's nakedness.

"You were about to say?" Fuzzy questioned, before she then pushed him on his back.

Before Speedy got the chance to answer, Fuzzy mounted

him and began to take him on the ride of his life.

10

Two Years Later

"**You** sure you don't mind watching the kids for Speedy and me?" Fuzzy asked as she packed up Sadé and Junior's overnight bags.

"Girl, please!" Red waved her off. "They are going to be doing me a big favor, 'cause once they run that bad-ass son of mine to death, he's gonna be out for the night," she laughed as she gave Fuzzy a high five.

The past two years had been hard on Red, not financially but mentally and physically, raising a son without Menace around, even though Speedy helped out as much as he could. After Fuzzy gathered up and finished getting everything the kids needed for the night, she went to the back door, stuck her head out, and then called them in: "Time to go to Aunt Red's place!"

The kids all sprinted to the door. Little Menace fell at least three times before he made it. When they were all seated in their car seats, Fuzzy waved them off. Speedy walked up behind Fuzzy as she stood in the doorway and watched Red back out of the driveway.

"Bye, Mommy!" Junior called out, waving his little hand from side to side excitedly.

Over the past year, Junior had come out of his shy stage around Fuzzy and started calling her "Mommy," and she happily called him "Son" in return. At times Sadé would become a little jealous of the attention Fuzzy showed him, but Speedy would come along and change all of that by showering her with all of her favorite gifts. That was the first time Speedy felt like his family was complete.

"You ready?" he asked as he slid on his four-finger ring with his name spelled across the front.

He knew he was going to be the center of attention in his red and off-white MCM suit. Tonight was the night Speedy and Fuzzy were throwing their old school/throwback jamboree party, and he couldn't wait to see all the people he was sure were going to be in attendance.

"Let me see. Ummmm!" Fuzzy inspected her money-green and white Adidas suit with a matching pair of shell toes.

After reaching up and sliding Speedy's chain up over his head and putting it around her neck, she replied, "Now I'm ready!"

Speedy watched her skip to the car and jump behind the wheel of the new, all-black Drophead Coupe that he had bought her for an anniversary gift.

"You coming or what?" she asked once she started the engine.

Speedy shook his head, hopped off the porch, and then jogged to the car and got in.

On the way to their club, all Speedy could think about was how much he wished his partner was there with him. So much had happened over the last two years. Money was still coming in. As matter of fact, more money was coming in now. Tank had bought his first house, and Lil Man and his girlfriend had just had a little boy, who they named Lucky in memory of his cousin.

When Fuzzy pulled her Rolls-Royce in front of the club, everyone stopped whatever it was they were doing and stood at attention and waited for them to step out. Since visiting the 40/40, Speedy had stepped up his club game and had a red carpet rolled out for all the elite members of the club to walk down. As soon as Speedy's and Fuzzy's feet hit the ground, they were guarded and escorted down the carpet. They greeted all of their friends and partygoers with waves or handshakes before they finally made it to the door.

"The couple of the year!" DJ Ollie B screamed into the microphone when they entered the front door.

They felt like the first man and woman as the crowd showed their respect with howls and whistles from all around them. On the way to the elevator, Speedy made a couple of stops to holler at a few major figures in the game.

"Who were those two guys with the two men guarding them?" Fuzzy asked, once they approached the elevator.

Speedy turned around to see who she was talking about and immediately recognized Mark and Alex. After explaining how he knew them, he broke down who the two men standing on each side of them were.

"The brown-skinned cat with the dreads is named Lamont. Mark pulled him into the clique once he saved his life, and the light-skinned cat standing on the other side of them is their cousin, the Infamous Romeo."

Fuzzy was about to ask what made people refer to the pretty boy as infamous, until Speedy gave her a knowing look with his eyebrows raised. He then turned back around and pressed the number two on the elevator panel. She nodded her head in understanding and then glanced over at the two men. She then looked off at the dimly lit VIP booth in the far corner.

"And who are they?" she pointed at the two guys ducked off behind tinted shades.

Speedy turned back around as the elevator made its way to the ground floor, and squinted his eyes, trying to focus through all the smoke and partygoers in attendance. He smiled when he laid eyes on his friend from his old hood.

"Oh, that's my man Hadji," he answered, and then looked at the guy next to him. "That's his cousin, Sean, sitting beside him."

Just as Speedy was about to go speak to them, he stopped in his tracks.

"And who's that?" Fuzzy asked as another guy walked up with a bottle of Moet in his hand and took a seat.

Fuzzy noticed Speedy's body tense up, and she immediately adjusted her Derringer under her jacket.

What the fuck is that nigga Gee doing with them? he wondered.

"Babe!" Fuzzy called out, snapping Speedy from his

thoughts. "You okay?"

"Yeah, I'm good," he answered, just as the elevator doors slid open.

"Come on then," she whispered as she grabbed his hand.

He made a mental note to pull Hadji's coattail on the company that he was keeping in his circle. As Speedy backpedaled into the elevator, his eyes locked with Gee's. A cold chill ran up and down his spine when Gee held up his bottle in Speedy's direction and then smiled. As soon as the door to the elevator closed behind them, Fuzzy began with her questions. After Speedy finished explaining to her who Gee (Greedy) was and how he had killed his very own blood brother to get his connect, the elevator buzzed, indicating they had reached their floor.

When Speedy and Fuzzy exited on the second floor, everything changed. Even though the music stayed the same and the elite members were also dressed in old-school attire, the atmosphere was totally different. Speedy smiled from ear to ear as he inhaled the smell of new and old money all around him. Instead of wearing the cheap knock-off versions of clothes and jewelry, everything the elite members wore was authentic or custom made. As they scanned the elite VIP room, Fuzzy's gaze landed on a set of identical twins.

"Who are they?" she asked, pointing over to the bar area.

When Speedy spotted who she was talking about, he couldn't believe his eyes. "That's Malek and Maleki," Speedy answered, just as they looked in their direction.

When their eyes meet Speedy's, they both gave a salute in acknowledgement. Speedy did the same, and Fuzzy waved. She knew they had to be very important in some kind of way, because they were by far the life of the party. They both wore custom-made linen Gucci pant sets instead of the usual sports attire everyone else sported.

As Speedy and Fuzzy stepped off to see who else was in attendance, he began to tell her a story of how he knew the twins.

"Menace and I used to cop work from the twins. It was like they just jumped on the scene with made work, but only fucked with a handful of people that they trusted. Word on the streets at the time was they robbed an Arabian drug lord and took him for everything he was worth."

Fuzzy looked on in amazement as she listened. She couldn't believe the baby-faced cuties were stone-cold killers.

"Don't let the looks fool you," Speedy stated, reading Fuzzy's mind.

She shook her head in agreement because she knew the statement to be true, because she had fooled plenty of victims in her line of work. Before she could ask her final question, Speedy beat her to it once again.

"They beat the murder charge. The wife of their older brother, C.J., was the lawyer, and his adopted parents were the lawyer and the judge."

"Wow!" Fuzzy managed to say. "Look!" Fuzzy pointed

as they approached the last booth in the VIP section of the room. "What are you doing here?" Fuzzy asked her uncle Slim.

Slim stood to his feet and kissed Fuzzy on each cheek before giving her a big hug.

"I know you didn't think I was going to miss the biggest event of the year, did you?" Slim teased. "Sit," Slim gestured to them to take a seat at his booth.

"It's an honor to have you here with us tonight," Speedy admitted as they both took their seats. "Do you need anything?"

Slim looked over at Speedy as if to say he already had everything a man could wish for. "Well, there is one thing!" Slim smiled and then looked over at the bar, where two Brazilian twins dressed in matching Fila suits sat.

Speedy glanced over at them to see to whom Slim was referring.

"Done!" Speedy leaned over in Fuzzy's direction and

whispered in her ear.

They watched as Fuzzy went over to approach the twins, and within a minute flat, they were all making their way back over to the booth. Once introductions were made, Speedy and Fuzzy stood to their feet so they could finish making their rounds.

"Well, Unc, we have to be going back downstairs to tend to our other guests now. I'll call you first thing in the morning to check up on you."

Slim nodded his head and then held up his bottle of Dom to the sky. Before Speedy and Fuzzy reached the elevator, she took one last look back at her uncle, who was sandwiched between the twins with a big smile on his face. She knew they were in for a big surprise when they left the club with Slim.

Speedy's favorite old-school jam, *Just to Get a Rep* by legendary rapper Gang Starr, blasted through the speakers as he stood with his back against the bar and looked around at the sea of people on the dance floor. He never would have imagined in a million years that he would be so successful, not only in the underground world, but on the business side of things as well. He looked over to his left and spotted Fuzzy mingling with a few of her friends from her old neighborhood. When she looked up, she caught her husband staring at her and wondered what was going through his mind at the time.

"I love you," she mouthed the words, before licking her lips teasingly.

"I love you more," he mouthed back, followed by blowing her a kiss.

After she caught it, she kissed her hand and placed it to her heart. That was a game they always played. However, for some strange reason, her smile turned into a frown and fear replaced her once happy features. She began to force her way through the crowd in an attempt to get over to him. It seemed to Speedy like everything was moving in slow motion as he tried to figure out what was going on. He could no longer hear the thunderous bass from the speakers, only the lyrics and Fuzzy screaming his name. From his peripheral, he could see a dark figure moving swiftly in his direction with a foreign object in his hand. Out of instinct, Speedy dropped his bottle of champagne and reached for his gun that he had in his waistline.

"Some brothers gotta go out just to get a rep!" was the only thing Speedy heard, followed by a single gunshot, before his body went crashing down to the floor.

Everyone in Club Drama began to trample over each other in an attempt to get away from the gunfire. When the shooter stepped closer into view, Speedy knew the reason he was lying in a puddle of his own blood.

"I knew I should've killed you a long time ago," he managed to say as he choked on his blood. *If Menace was alive right now, he would be saying, "I told you so,"* Speedy thought to himself as K-Rock hovered over him with a smoking gun in his hand.

Speedy knew his reign at the top was over when he looked into the young killer's eyes, and his life began to flash before him—his wedding day, the day Fuzzy gave birth to Sadé, the day he picked Menace up from rehab, and the day he counted his first million. His heart rate began to decrease. The thought of losing his best friend and crime partner, his baby mama, and now his life all crossed his mind in the blink of an eye.

"This is for my brother J.B., you pussy-ass nigga," K-Rock screamed, before emptying the entire clip into Speedy's chest.

He watched Speedy's body jerk and twist until he lay there motionless, before spitting in his face. K-Rock was so zoned out, he never noticed Fuzzy behind him until she pressed the barrel of her Derringer to his head. Before he could turn around, she pulled back on both of the triggers and sent both bullets to his brain, just like her Uncle Slim had taught her.

"Please don't leave us, Speedy," she begged, once she

bent down and cradled his head in her arms.

Speedy's glassy eyes stared back up at her, but Fuzzy knew he was gone. She reached down and closed them before kissing the top of his head.

"I'll always love you," she promised as Slim walked up behind her, took her gun, and then handed it to one of his bodyguards.

They headed to the back door exit where Slim's bodyguard had his triple black Bentley Mulsanne waiting for them.

For the next few days, Fuzzy stayed buried in her room with the curtains drawn shut. Slim had taken care of all of the funeral arrangements, and thanks to Red taking Sadé and Junior to her house, she had peace and quiet. If it wasn't for Slim sending his chef over to cook breakfast, lunch, and diner, Fuzzy didn't know how she would have made it through, even though she barely ate a thing. Due to the fact that she was so used to Speedy running things in the house and in the drug game, she didn't know what she should do now that he was gone. One thing she did know for certain: She was not staying in North Carolina any longer.

~ ~ ~

After Speedy's funeral, everyone met back at Fuzzy's restaurant, Big Mama's Kitchen, for his celebration.

"Girl, what are you doing up here all by yourself? You should be downstairs entertaining everyone." Red pranced into the office with a flute filled to the top with Moscato in it. She and everyone else in the building had been searching for Fuzzy for the past thirty minutes. Red walked over to Fuzzy and gave her a big hug and a kiss on the cheek.

After their short embrace, Fuzzy put on a weak smile. "I had to come up here for a minute and get myself together," she answered, once she took a step back and wiped her eyes.

Red hated seeing her best friend in such a depressed state. She couldn't find the words to cheer her up, so she was glad when she heard their favorite song.

"Come on, girl. This our jam!" Red said excitedly as she grabbed Fuzzy by her hand and led the way out of her office.

When they got downstairs, Red dragged Fuzzy to the dance floor, where they danced the night away.

"Can I have this dance?" Fuzzy heard a familiar voice call out behind her. "How you holding up?" Slim asked, once she turned around and placed her hand in his.

"Okay, I guess," she answered. "I just miss him so much already."

"I know you do. He was a good man."

Before they could get too deep into their conversation, Fuzzy felt a light tug at her waist.

"I wanna dance, Mommy," Junior smiled, looking up at her.

Looking down into his eyes immediately made hers water. They reminded her of Speedy so much. She didn't know how she would ever get over him with Junior in her life.

"Come on, baby boy." Fuzzy grabbed Junior's little hands

and placed them in hers and began to two-step.

Slim looked over toward Fuzzy's table and saw Sadé sitting with Red, so he decided to go over and see if his grand-niece wanted to dance.

"Can I have this dance, princess?"

Sadé hopped down from her seat, placed her hand in Slim's, and then pulled him to the dance floor beside Fuzzy and Junior. Before long, Fuzzy, Junior, Slim, and Sadé were in an all-out dance contest. Everyone stopped what they were doing and made a huge circle around the four as they did their thing. People in the crew began to make it rain on the dance machines, Sadé and Junior. After the contest was over, the partygoers declared Sadé and Junior the winners.

As the celebration came to an end, Lil Man and Tank approached Fuzzy to say their goodbyes.

"I want to thank you for all you've done for me and the crew," Lil Man told her.

"You mean what Speedy did for you and the crew," Fuzzy

corrected.

Before he could respond, Tank cut in: "If there's anything you or the kids need, just holla. We got y'all."

Fuzzy looked at the sincerity in their eyes and immediately realized why Speedy and Menace pulled them into the crew.

"I will," she assured them.

Tank said a few more kind words before heading to the exit to pull the car up front for Lil Man.

"Well, I guess this is it!" Lil Man went into his pocket and pulled out a small brown envelope.

"What is this for?" Fuzzy asked, with a confused look on her face.

When she opened it, there was $25,000 inside.

"I owed that to Speedy before he died," Lil Man answered.

Fuzzy closed the envelope and handed it back to him, and then wiped the tear that had formed in the corner of her eye.

"Believe me, Lil Man, he would've wanted you to have it."

He tried to decline, but Fuzzy insisted.

"Me and Speedy had a serious talk before he passed, and I know he wasn't the real head of our crew!" Lil Man let it be known that Speedy had told him Fuzzy was the real queen pin behind their crew.

Fuzzy thought long and hard before she spoke. "I'll have someone get in contact with you tomorrow."

After noticing that Lil Man's facial expression never changed, she knew she was making the right choice by putting him in charge. Anyone else would have been excited to get the position of the HNIC, but Lil Man proved to be humble, and that's what Fuzzy needed. But to be sure, she had to ask, "You sure you're ready for this?"

"I was born ready," Lil Man responded.

No more words needed to be said as Fuzzy watched him make his exit. Fuzzy called Slim's limo driver to pull up front so she and the kids could go home. To her surprise, Slim was at the back of the limo door waiting for Fuzzy. After the kids were placed inside sound asleep, Slim got right down to business.

"So, have you made a decision yet?"

Fuzzy took in a deep breath and then exhaled before responding. "Lil Man's the one," she answered confidently.

She sat nervously watching her uncle's facial expression. She was always known for being a good judge of character, but she knew Slim was much better at it, so his approval meant the world to her.

"Well, Lil Man it is!" Slim agreed.

He had also done a background check, and if he would have had to make the decision Fuzzy had, he would have picked the same man. If not Lil Man, he would have chosen Tank.

Fuzzy smiled and then rested her head against the headrest and closed her eyes. Only time would tell if Lil Man would be able to handle the half ton of product Fuzzy had in store for him.

11

"**Hurry** up, girl!" Red yelled from the driver's side window of her Cayenne as she watched Fuzzy load the last suitcase into the back of her G55.

"Because I'm not trying to get caught up in all that traffic on I-95," she claimed as Little Menace continuously kicked on the back of her seat in an attempt to get her to start driving.

"Hey!" she shouted, after reaching around behind her and popping him on the legs twice.

"Leave my god son alone," Fuzzy called out in Little Menace's defense, once she turned around and caught Red in the act.

Red looked at her best friend, sucked her teeth, and then rolled her eyes. "Whatever," she replied, giving Fuzzy the hand.

Red rolled up her window and turned the A/C on full

blast. She then turned on Little Menace's favorite cartoon on the DVD player.

Fuzzy made her way to the driver's door of her truck and climbed in. "Y'all ready?" she asked Sadé and Junior, when she looked in the rearview mirror at her two bundles of joy waiting patiently for her to start the truck so they could watch a movie.

Once they nodded their heads, Fuzzy dug into her handbag to retrieve her keys. "Damn!" she cursed herself, when she realized she had left her keys on the key rack in the hall. She climbed back out of the truck and flagged Red to get her attention. "I forgot my keys," she yelled, once Red rolled down her window, and then she ran back up to the house.

"Girl, I swear, if your head wasn't attached to your body, you'd forget that sometimes," Red joked as Fuzzy made her way into the house.

"Stop, boy!" Fuzzy heard Red scream at Little Menace as the door closed behind her.

"I must have left them in the bedroom," Fuzzy said to

herself as she looked at the empty spot on the key rack where her key usually sat.

She quickly turned on her heels and ran upstairs taking two steps at a time until she made it to the top. Out of breath, Fuzzy made it to her room and burst through the door.

"There they are!"

She rushed over to the dresser and picked them up. As soon as she turned around to head back downstairs, she was hit by a sharp pain in her head, and then everything went blank.

When Fuzzy finally came to, she rubbed the small knot that had formed on the top of her head.

"What happened?" she questioned as she looked around and tried to focus on her surroundings.

"You had a little accident," she heard a voice call out behind her.

Fuzzy tried to remember where she had seen the light-skinned female, once her face came clear into vision. The migraine was making it a little harder to do, not to mention the fact that the female had a small caliber gun in her face.

"Who are you, and what are you doing in my house?" Fuzzy asked, wanting to get to the bottom of things.

The female looked at her with a confused expression on her face before she replied, "You really don't remember me, do you?"

Fuzzy squinted her eyes and tried to get a closer look at the woman in front of her. She looked very familiar, but Fuzzy couldn't quite put her finger on it.

"Let me help you out a little," the female offered before continuing. "I was the one dancing on Speedy at the grand opening of his club."

As soon as the words left her mouth, Fuzzy instantly remembered the pretty girl who was all up on Speedy that night, and became enraged.

"Uh, uh, uh," Marie warned as she clicked the hammer back on the .22 revolver that she held in her hand. "I wouldn't do that if I were you."

Fuzzy wanted to kick herself in the ass for letting Slim

take her gun from her the night Speedy got killed. All she could do now was wait for the perfect opportunity so she could make her move, if she intended on making it out of there alive.

"Or should I go back a little further for you?" Marie went on.

Fuzzy sat patiently and listened to what Marie had to say as thoughts of survival ran through her head.

"Do you remember when you caught your husband cheating on you at the Marriott?" she asked, snapping Fuzzy out of her thoughts.

This broad really must have gotten me confused or is completely insane, Fuzzy thought to herself, because she had never caught Speedy cheating on her.

Marie could tell Fuzzy was lost, but she was sure to refresh her memory for her. "I know it's been a while, but think back to when you were in college and came home for the weekend for a surprise visit."

Fuzzy remembered that night very well. It was the night

she drove home from college to tell King she was pregnant. As soon as she hit the Wilson city limits, she spotted King's car at the hotel and pulled in. When she stepped in the hotel lobby, she saw King walking in her direction on his phone with a big smile on his face, which suddenly disappeared once he saw her. No sooner than he hung up on the person on the other end had Fuzzy jumped dead on him.

"I knew you looked familiar that night at the club for some reason," Fuzzy said out loud, not believing she hadn't recognized the woman.

She remembered her walking through the lobby as King tried to rush her out to her car to stop her from making an even bigger scene. What was puzzling Fuzzy at the time was why Marie was at her house now, since both Speedy and King were dead.

"I know what you're wondering," Marie leaned in and whispered into Fuzzy's ear. "Let's just say there's an old saying that if you can't get to someone, get the closest one to them. Have you ever heard of that?"

Fuzzy cringed as a chill ran down her spine. She knew the saying all too well, because she lived by the same code herself.

"You see. Speedy killed my baby daddy, King."

Fuzzy couldn't believe her ears.

"Don't look surprised, sweetheart. King and I had been fucking for years. As a matter of fact, we started right after you went off to college," Marie bragged. "After doing a little investigation, I found out that Speedy didn't have King killed that day his Bentley got shot up. It was you who put the hit out on him."

"The reason I wanted Speedy and Menace dead was because they killed my father. Do you remember a detective named Joey Russo?" Marie questioned with tears in her eyes.

Fuzzy watched Marie's hands as they began to shake out of control. She just hoped Marie didn't pull back on the trigger by mistake. Marie spoke up, breaking Fuzzy out of her thoughts.

"That was me and Liz's father they killed to beat

Menace's drug charge. They killed him right outside of our house in the driveway. We saw them with our own eyes, and vowed not to tell anyone and to get revenge for what they did to him. The only other person that knew about it was his partner, Detective Branch, who your uncle Slim killed."

"Me and Liz almost had Speedy and Menace the night of the grand opening of y'all's club, and if it wasn't for Liz being in the truck the night Menace killed her baby daddy, J.B., she would still be alive," Marie claimed, before wiping her eyes and continuing. "And now it's time to pay the piper."

"Fuck them! They all got what they deserved!" Fuzzy shouted, with hate in her eyes.

Fuzzy jumped to her feet, but before she could swing a blow, Marie hit her in the side of her face, momentarily dazing her.

"Damn, bitch! What's taking you so long?" Red shouted as she burst through the door, catching Marie by surprise.

When Marie turned to face the door, that was the opportunity Fuzzy had been waiting on. She threw a wild haymaker that caught Marie dead on her chin and buckled her knees, making her drop the gun out of her hand. Before Marie could hit the floor, she grabbed Fuzzy and they tumbled down together. With Fuzzy having a slight weight advantage, she was able to get on top of Marie and began to rain down a fury of punches to her face. The only thing that saved her was that one of Fuzzy's blows landed on the hardwood floor. Marie rolled her over and began to get the best of her. It wasn't until Red picked up the gun and sent a bullet to the back of Marie's head that she stopped. Once Fuzzy moved Marie's lifeless body off the top of her, she stood to her feet and looked at her best friend.

"I'm glad you came when you did," Fuzzy said while walking up to her.

Just as she got close to her, Red lifted her arm up and placed the barrel of the gun to the center of her forehead.

"What you doing?" Fuzzy asked out of disbelief as she stared into Red's teary eyes. "Put the gun down," she pleaded.

"You just don't get it, do you?"

"Get what, Red?" Fuzzy asked, confused.

"All of our lives you have had it all. The clothes, the men, the money, and a family that loved you. I've always been in your shadow," Red cried. "But not anymore!"

She wiped the tears from her eyes.

"That's not true, Red. My family always treated you like a part of the family. I've always treated you like a sister. So what are you talking about?"

"That's the problem. I got whatever you wanted me to have. What about what I wanted for myself," Red shouted. "You didn't even want Speedy at first. It was me that influenced you to talk to him. Why didn't you give him to me if you didn't want him?"

Fuzzy couldn't believe what she was hearing. "So that's what this is about? Speedy?" Fuzzy asked as she began to sob.

"Speedy, King, the list goes on. You always get the good ones, and all I get is their friends. What is it that you got that I don't? All I wanted was to be loved. Why don't no one want to take care of me like they did you?" Red wanted to know.

"What? I know this ain't about money. You can have the money. Here!" Fuzzy offered as she handed her the keys to one of the storage rooms in which she and Speedy kept money.

"There's a little over $1,000,000 in cash in it. You can have it."

Fuzzy looked in Red's eyes and saw the same look she had seen so many times before. That's when she knew she wouldn't be leaving the room alive.

"Take care of my kids for me," Fuzzy begged as the hand that Red held the gun in began to shake.

All she saw before she closed her eyes to be reunited with her father and Speedy was Red's finger pulling back on the trigger and the hammer about to be released.

Bang!

"You okay?" Slim asked as he stepped over Red's lifeless body and then held Fuzzy in his arms.

Fuzzy opened her eyes and held on to her uncle as tight as she could. She couldn't believe she was blinded to Red's jealousy all those years.

"The kids," she screamed as she jumped to her feet.

Before she could make it out of the room, Slim informed her that they were taken to his house by one of his bodyguards. Slim pulled out his cell and pressed down on number one until a familiar voice answered.

"I need you to send the clean-up crew over to Speed—I mean Fuzzy's place," Slim ordered.

"They're on the way," Ben assured him before ending the call.

Slim walked up to his niece and put his arm around her shoulder and then walked her out of the room.

"How did you know to come by the house?" Fuzzy asked as they headed downstairs.

Slim looked down at her and then smiled.

"You know I couldn't let you go down south without your baby," Slim replied as he held Fuzzy's two-shot Dillinger in the palm of his hand.

He had just had his gunsmith replace the barrel on it, so

K-Rock's murder couldn't be linked back to her. But now he had to have it done again. When they walked out of the front door, Fuzzy noticed that Red's Porsche truck was gone.

"You can stop by the house and get the kids on your way to Georgia."

Fuzzy hated the fact that she was leaving the house. So many memories had been made over the years. She vowed to never sell it due to the fact it was Speedy's parents' house.

"Thank you, Uncle."

Fuzzy hopped in the truck, and within an hour, she and the kids were on their way to start a new life where they were no longer a royal family. They would simply be everyday people, until Fuzzy decided to resurface.

One Year Later

Shelia sold her spot house in the hood and finally decided to check herself into rehab. Upon her release, Fuzzy was waiting for her with open arms. Fuzzy also had the deed to Big Mama's Kitchen as well as the deed to the condo that she and Red shared before she moved in with Speedy. She made a promise to Speedy before he died that she would take good care of the family if anything ever happened to him, and Shelia was considered a part of their family.

Lil Man was running things with an iron fist, just the way Speedy and Menace would have wanted it run themselves. Every once and a while, Lil Man and a few of the crew members would go down to Atlanta and check up on Fuzzy and the kids. Lil Man even thought about expanding the family business down in the South as well.

Tank was blessed with Club Drama, and, of course, he kept the old-school jamboree going once a year in memory of Speedy. A gigantic picture of Speedy and Menace covered the back wall of the club as the backdrop for taking pictures.

Slim was the same cool, slick, and flamboyant OG he had always been, and he continued to hold down the city's drug trade and run things.

After Fuzzy relocated to Georgia, she kept a low profile. She took some of her money and opened up a nice upscale club in the heart of Atlanta. Even though Red had crossed her in the end, every time Fuzzy would go to North Carolina, she would go to Red's grave site and update her on how things were going with her and the kids, and reminisce on the good old days that they had shared together. No matter how things may have turned out between the two of them, Red would always be connected to a special place in Fuzzy's heart.

Text Good2Go at 31996 to receive new release updates via text message

BOOKS BY GOOD2GO AUTHORS

GOOD 2 GO FILMS PRESENTS

WRONG PLACE WRONG TIME WEB SERIES

**NOW AVAILABLE ON
GOOD2GOFILMS.COM & YOUTUBE
SUBSCRIBE TO THE CHANNEL**

**THE HAND I WAS DEALT WEB SERIES
NOW AVAILABLE ON YOUTUBE!**

**THE HAND I WAS DEALT SEASON TWO
NOW AVAILABLE ON YOUTUBE!**

THE HACKMAN
NOW AVAILABLE ON YOUTUBE!

FILMS